"Aren't you forgetting something?"

Cheska's mind was a blank.

"The kiss," Lawson said, walking toward her.

"Kiss?" Cheska queried.

"You know the saying 'kiss and make up'?" Lawson bent over her. "We've done the making up part, so...?"

"Funny you should mention it," she said. "I was just thinking the same thing myself."

Lawson straightened a little, his eyes suddenly watchful. "You were?"

ELIZABETH OLDFIELD's writing career started as a teenage hobby, when she had articles published. However, on her marriage the creative instinct was diverted into the production of a daughter and son. A decade later, when her husband's job took them to Singapore, she resumed writing, and had her first romance novel accepted in 1982. Now she's hooked on the genre! They live in London, and Elizabeth travels widely to authenticate the background of her books.

Books by Elizabeth Oldfield

Don't miss any of our special offers. Write to us at the following address for information on our newest releases.

Harlequin Reader Service
U.S.: 3010 Walden Ave., P.O. Box 1325, Buffalo, NY 14269
Canadian: P.O. Box 609, Fort Erie, Ont. L2A 5X3

ELIZABETH OLDFIELD
Dark Victory

Harlequin Books

TORONTO • NEW YORK • LONDON
AMSTERDAM • PARIS • SYDNEY • HAMBURG
STOCKHOLM • ATHENS • TOKYO • MILAN
MADRID • WARSAW • BUDAPEST • AUCKLAND

If you purchased this book without a cover you should be aware
that this book is stolen property. It was reported as "unsold and
destroyed" to the publisher, and neither the author nor the
publisher has received any payment for this "stripped book."

ISBN 0-373-11800-7

DARK VICTORY

First North American Publication 1996.

Copyright © 1994 by Elizabeth Oldfield.

All rights reserved. Except for use in any review, the reproduction or
utilization of this work in whole or in part in any form by any electronic,
mechanical or other means, now known or hereafter invented, including
xerography, photocopying and recording, or in any information storage
or retrieval system, is forbidden without the written permission of the
publisher, Harlequin Enterprises Limited, 225 Duncan Mill Road,
Don Mills, Ontario, Canada M3B 3K9.

All characters in this book have no existence outside the imagination of
the author and have no relation whatsoever to anyone bearing the same
name or names. They are not even distantly inspired by any individual
known or unknown to the author, and all incidents are pure invention.

This edition published by arrangement with Harlequin Books S.A.

® and ™ are trademarks of the publisher. Trademarks indicated with
® are registered in the United States Patent and Trademark Office, the
Canadian Trade Marks Office and in other countries.

Printed in U.S.A.

CHAPTER ONE

CHESKA sauntered contentedly towards the woodland pool which, from childhood, she had always regarded as her own special place. It felt so *good* to be home. Especially when the sky stretched above in a cloudless blue, when a warm breeze stirred the leaves in the trees, when the countryside was bright with drifts of wild flowers. She hugged slender arms around herself. It felt so good to be alone in the tranquillity of the morning and, praise be, to have at last escaped from the unfortunate, pressurising, increasingly dangerous attentions of——

Her thoughts and her footsteps came to a full stop. Her contentment vanished. She was *not* alone. On the far side of the oval pool, a man lay on his stomach, half hidden in the long grass. Cheska's pewter-grey eyes narrowed. Who was he? What did he want? He appeared to be gazing up the long sweeping slope of green lawns in the direction of the manor house, but why? She regarded him with suspicion and acute distaste. She did not appreciate anyone violating her hideaway. After all, this was private property, she thought indignantly—and it had yet to reach eight o'clock.

Cheska studied the trespasser. Had she stumbled upon a gypsy, intending to poach a rabbit or maybe a wild deer? His thick jet-black hair and the golden skin of his arms made Romany blood a possibility.

Or might he be one of the so-called 'New Age' travellers the newspapers had been complaining about, scouting out a suitable tract of land on which his druggy friends could descend in hordes and create havoc by holding an illegal pop festival? Defiant hands were spread on her slim Lycra-clad hips. Over her dead body. Or was he, perhaps, more innocently, a tramp sleeping rough? Or, less threateningly still, a bird-watcher? All four options were dismissed. The tall, athletic figure stretched out on the far side of the sun-dappled water was too well dressed. He might be wearing jeans, but even from her vantage-point Cheska could see that they were clean and well cut, and that the burgundy sports shirt which fitted his muscular torso like a glove was of good quality.

Her eyes drifted back down. His lean-hipped, taut-curved backside was one of the sexiest she had ever seen. On a scale of one to ten, it definitely rated as a ten. Cheska gave her head a little shake. Where had that thought come from? The jet-lag which had kept her tossing and turning all night and had her raring to go at dawn must be befuddling her. She was not in the habit of admiring male bottoms and awarding points—let alone so early in the day—and, instead of admiring his, she ought to be deciding what the man was up to.

As Cheska watched, he slowly tilted his dark head from side to side, as though studying the eighteenth-century stone mansion from different angles, then he lifted a pair of binoculars. Her heart started to race. Oh, lord, what she had stumbled upon was a thief, undertaking a reconnaissance of the house before he broke in and swiped a selection of the family heirlooms! An exceptionally professional thief, she realised with galloping alarm, for a pad had been produced from his breast pocket and he had begun making notes.

With hasty steps Cheska backed out of sight behind the thick trunk of a beech tree. She gulped down a breath. What was she to do? Her instinct was to steal quietly and quickly away before the man spotted her, which, as he was so engrossed in his survey, should be simple. Her brow furrowed. Yet a prompt retreat would mean that, when she telephoned the police, there would be little description to give them—unless she waxed lyrical about his cute rear-end, Cheska thought wryly. But perhaps the thief was a known villain who, if identified, could be shadowed and apprehended. A burnished curl of cinnamon-brown hair was hooked decisively behind one ear. Before making her getaway, she would creep around the edge of the steep-sided pool and sneak a swift, discerning sideways look.

After checking that the trespasser remained preoccupied, Cheska left the beech tree and, with stealthy scampering steps, hightailed it to the leafy screen of a rhododendron. She slunk to another bush, and another, and the next. The note-making continued. A few more furtive prowls and she was on the point of taking up her viewing position beneath the convenient canopy of a weeping willow, when her prey reached down into the grass to produce a camera. As he half turned, Cheska froze. Her pewter-grey eyes flew open wide. Her heart thudded behind her ribs. Jet lag must be playing weird tricks again, for the glimpse she had had of

the man's strong, angled profile had made her
think... It *couldn't* be, a voice wailed in protest
inside her head. It *is*, her eyesight and common
sense insisted. That Roman nose and clean-cut
jawline are instantly recognisable, even after a gap
of five years. When the man twisted his torso and
reached down into the grass again, this time to dis-
pense with a lens cap, her fears were confirmed.
Her worst fears. Cheska raised a shaky hand to her
brow. She had never expected to meet Lawson
Giordano, whizz-kid director of television commercials, again, and certainly not in the depths of
the Sussex countryside in the early hours of a
summer morning.

She stared at the prone male figure. How did he
come to be here? she wondered frantically. What
on earth could he be doing? Her curiosity received
short shift. His activities did not matter. What
mattered was that Lawson Giordano had not seen
her, so she did not need to meet him *now*, Cheska
thought thankfully. She could, would, creep quickly
and quietly away. As he focused the camera she
took a blind step in hasty retreat, turned, and felt
her flip-flop sandal start to slide out from beneath
her foot. Her balance went.

'Aarrgh!' Cheska yelped, as in a flurry of wind-
milling arms, skidding legs and spiralling body she
slithered out from the weeping willow, down the
bank of the pool and into the dark green water.

Above her, Lawson Giordano's head whipped
round and he stared. He clambered to his feet.
'Francesca Rider?' he said, in stunned disbelief. For
a moment or two he gawked down at her, and then
he started to laugh.

Pink-faced and with untidy clouds of brown hair tumbling over her eyes, Cheska glared. A dry spring and summer had reduced the level of the pond, so the water barely reached her thighs and the legs of her black cycling shorts. She had also, by some miracle, managed to remain upright. And she was unhurt. She swept back her hair. OK, OK, she thought tetchily, her impromptu descent could be construed as somewhat comic, but she resented providing amusement for a man who had once savagely condemned her and then proceeded to exploit her for his own ends. Exploit her ruthlessly.

Cheska folded her arms across her chest. 'It isn't funny,' she declared, her voice frigid.

Although it required an effort and a moment or two, Lawson Giordano managed to clamp down on his laughter—though a crooked grin annoyingly remained.

'You think not?' he said.

'I do!' Cheska snapped. 'And it's your fault that I fell.'

'Mine?'

She glowered up at him. 'I didn't expect anyone to be here, and—and you startled me.'

Dark brown eyes made a swift but expert appraisal of her slim figure in the Lycra shorts and matching cut-away top.

'You thought I might be a lust-crazed rapist, scouring the fields for scantily dressed maidens and about to pounce?' Lawson Giordano suggested.

Cheska's glower intensified. She had not considered herself scantily dressed—until he had mentioned it. But now she felt like a fugitive from some Las Vegas strip show!

'You were looking at the house and I thought you might be what's commonly called "casing the joint",' she retorted, and realised he was staring.

Cheska flushed. In folding her arms, she had pushed up the high breasts which sprang from her narrow body and now the honeyed curves seemed in imminent danger of spilling from her low-cut neckline. Hastily dropping her arms, she waded two or three steps across the muddy floor of the pool to the side, but when she reached it she frowned. The bank, which was covered with ferns and stones and yellow wands of loosestrife, was almost vertical. How did she climb up it?

Looming above, Lawson Giordano made a tall silhouette against the dazzle of the morning light. 'May I give you a hand?' he offered, in the low, smoky voice which she remembered so well.

When he held down a golden-skinned arm covered with a floss of black hair, Cheska eyed it warily. She did not want to touch him. She did not want to have *any* physical contact with the man. No, thanks. Never again.

'I can manage on my own, thank you,' she informed him, with the grand hauteur of a duchess.

Lawson shook his head. 'You can't,' he said.

After undertaking a more detailed scrutiny of the bank, Cheska gave a silent scream. While she was loath to admit it, he seemed to be right. Her teeth ground together. She not only balked at touching him, she also objected to Lawson Giordano's taking control of the situation—as he had always been so magnificently in control of situations before. But what was the alternative? She was damned if she would scramble up to him on her hands and knees.

Cheska forced a grit-eating smile. 'I can't,' she agreed, and clasped the large hand which he had continued to hold down.

It would serve him right if, instead of him pulling her out, she pulled him in, Cheska reflected, as her rescuer planted his long legs apart and prepared to haul. A dipping would be no more than he deserved and apt punishment, in view of his laughter, and his cruel manipulation of her in the past. Indeed, nothing would give her greater satisfaction than to manipulate *him*, by jerking at his hand so that he hurtled past her down the bank, to splash headlong into the water. And if he should sink for the regulation three times—tough luck! She had no badges for life-saving.

'Don't even think about it,' Lawson warned.

Cheska was looking at him in astonishment, wondering if she had a plate glass forehead, when with one powerful pull he yanked her out of the water, up the ferny slope and on to the side. Her legs skitter-skattered like pistons until—wham!— she thudded up against the firm-muscled wall of his chest.

'Oh!' she gasped.

In reflex, she clutched at his shoulders, and in reflex his arms went around her waist. Breathing hard, they stood together, body pressed against body, eyes gazing into eyes.

'You always were a bloody-minded, uncooperative little bitch, and you haven't changed,' Lawson said roughly, then his dark head came down, blotting out the sun, and he kissed her.

Taken by surprise, Cheska opened her mouth to protest. That was her first mistake, for, as her lips parted, his tongue thrust between them, a predatory invader. Her second mistake was not to push him away. But how could she, when he had begun a seductive exploration of her mouth, when he was tasting her—and she was tasting him? A clean, male, intoxicating taste which revived all kinds of memories. As the kiss deepened, Cheska's head started to spin and her knees seemed to buckle. She clung tighter to his shoulders; it was vital if she was to remain upright. But clinging to him had been her third mistake, she realised, for when Lawson drew back a minute or two later he was smiling, a confident, amused, knowing smile.

'I—I have changed,' Cheska stammered, needing to break the spell which he seemed to have cast, desperate to stifle the frenetic thump-thump of her heart. Letting go of his shoulders, she placed her arms stiffly down by her sides. 'I have,' she repeated, her voice firmer this time.

A brow lifted. 'You're no longer susceptible?'

'Susceptible?' she queried. 'To what?'

Lawson traced the tip of a tapered index finger slowly across her bare midriff, leaving a trail of heat tingling in its wake.

'Me.'

Cheska took a brisk step in retreat. 'No way,' she said tartly.

'That wasn't the impression I received a moment ago.'

Her fingers curled into balls, their nails biting into her palms. She was furious with herself for having reacted so unthinkingly, so naïvely—and furious with him for daring to comment on it. It had seemed odd that Lawson Giordano should kiss her, but now she knew why. He had been testing her. He had been checking whether the sexual fire which he had once ignited with such casual ease could still be coaxed into flame. And she had obligingly boosted his male ego by providing the answer!

'You always were an arrogant bastard and you haven't changed,' Cheska declared, in a sharp reworking of his earlier condemnation of her.

At the back of her mind, it registered that he had not changed physically, either. His hair was still black and wavy, worn a mite too long for fashion and curling over his shirt collar. His eyes continued to be heavy-lidded and a lustrous yellow-flecked brown. His mouth remained...well, beautiful. The granite-cut upper lip hinted at imperiousness, the lower was full and sensual. Cheska felt an irritating and totally unwelcome *frisson*. Five years ago, his dark Latin looks and muscular physique had meant that Lawson Giordano had been almost insolently masculine. He still was.

'You're saying you're not susceptible?' he drawled.

'I'm saying that the only reason you weren't kicked on the shins just now, or kneed in the groin,' she added, with a razor of a smile, 'was because you took me unawares.'

Lawson moved his shoulders in a leisurely shrug. 'I was taught never to contradict a lady—even when she's lying through her teeth. But what are you doing here?' he went on, not missing a beat. 'How come you're wandering through the woods alone before breakfast, wearing a revealing top, and——' dark eyes dipped momentarily down to her hips in the elasticated shorts '—no knickers?'

Cheska forced herself to meet his steady gaze with an equally steady one of her own. He might just have got the better of her, but he would not be allowed to do so again. Whatever he said, whatever he did, she refused to be fazed. She would let him know that the gauche, biddable girl of so long ago had become a sophisticated and self-assured young woman.

'It was hot,' she declared, tossing back her mane of long brown hair in a couldn't-care-less gesture.

'And you don't wear knickers when it's hot?' The corner of his mouth tweaked. 'Now that's intriguing.'

Cheska jabbed a hand up the rolling lawn to where the windows of the house reflected the pale yellow of the morning sun. She had absolutely no wish to continue this discussion about her underwear—or lack of it.

'I'm here because Hatchford Manor is my home,' she said.

'Your home?' There was a long moment of silence before Lawson next spoke. 'But I understood that Rupert Finch, the owner, lived there alone. Apart from a housekeeper and her husband.'

'He does, most of the time—but I arrived back yesterday. Rupert is my brother.'

Lawson seemed to recoil in shock. 'Brother?' he repeated.

Cheska cast him a puzzled glance. She had never seen him thrown before, but his voice had been filled with horror and his tense expression made it plain that he was now working his way through all manner of difficulties and doubts. Yet why should the relationship be of any possible concern, pose any possible problem, to him?

'But he's Finch and you're Rider,' Lawson protested, raking back the strands of black hair which fell over his forehead. 'Besides, the guy's in his early fifties whereas you can only be . . . twenty-five?'

'Twenty-six,' Cheska amended. 'To be accurate, Rupert's my stepbrother, hence our different names and the gap in ages, but we're close and I always think of him as my brother.'

'So you're not blood relations,' he said, with what could be recognised as blatant relief.

She shook her head. 'His father married my mother. He married her late in life after his first wife, Rupert's mother, died. And my mother was a widow,' she explained.

'When we were talking last week, he did make a reference to a "Cheska",' Lawson recalled, frowning, 'but I thought he said you were abroad.'

'I was, until yesterday. However, I quit my job unexpectedly——' a shadow crossed her face '—and——'

'You were *working* abroad?' he cut in.

'What did you think I was doing, holidaying at length in glitzy abandon?' Cheska demanded. 'Cruising the Caribbean or living it up at a house party on the Côte d'Azur?'

'Something like that.' His eyes flickered over her. 'After all, you have a deep tan which couldn't have been acquired overnight, so——'

'Although I may have tended to swan around once, I now work hard for my living,' she informed him curtly.

'But you're no longer a model?'

'No, I stopped modelling shortly after we last met. To continue, I quit my job and——'

'You got fed up with it?' Lawson suggested.

Cheska's lips compressed. His question appeared to imply that she was both capricious and fickle.

'On the contrary, I was deeply interested in what I was doing and I would've stayed, but there were——' she hesitated '—problems. However, they were not of my making. Difficult though you may find this to believe, even "wilful little brats" grow up some time,' she said, tersely recalling a phrase which he had once used to describe her.

Brown eyes locked on to hers. 'Grow up into what—wilful big ones?'

She glared, so incensed by the insult which hung palpably in the air that she itched to slap his lean face. Slap it hard. Slap it ringingly. But, once again, Lawson Giordano had read what was in her mind.

'Try it, and you'll find yourself back in the water,' he warned.

'The speed of my departure meant I was only able to phone Rupert at the last minute,' Cheska said, tautly resuming her recital, 'so when he collected me from Heathrow late last night he'd had less than twenty-four hours' notice of my return.' She gave him a cold, unsmiling look. 'And what is the reason for *your* presence?'

'I'm doing preparatory work before I start filming.'

Her forehead crinkled. 'You're filming here, at Hatchford Manor?'

'I am,' Lawson said, bending to retrieve the binoculars, the camera and his notebook from the long grass. He straightened. 'I came yesterday and everyone else rolls up on Monday.'

Cheska's thoughts shattered. She had been looking forward to some peace and quiet in which to unwind and recover from the episode abroad, but there would be no quiet if a commercial was being made on the doorstep, and no peace of mind so long as the tall Italian remained in her vicinity. None.

'Rupert never said,' she objected, a mite pugnaciously.

'If you only arrived back late last night, I dare say he didn't have time to get around to it.'

'I guess not,' Cheska muttered.

Her stepbrother had not had much opportunity to tell her, never mind the time, she acknowledged ruefully. Yesterday evening, she had chattered non-stop about what had been happening in her life, while the fond bachelor had indulgently listened. As usual. Cheska frowned. Though she had not told him *everything*.

'The idea of filming offends you?' Lawson enquired, noticing her frown.

'No, but——'

'Your stepbrother's signature on the dotted line means the arrangement is incontrovertible,' he rasped, 'so if you should be toying with the idea of trying to talk him out of it you're wasting your time.'

'Am I? Well, let me tell you that if I did try to talk him out of it I'd manage it,' Cheska retorted. 'Rupert is prone to seeing things *my* way.'

'In which case, I'd sue for breach of contract. However, I'd advise you to remember that what I expect, I get.' His dark eyes were unblinking beneath straight black brows. 'Am I making myself clear?'

'Crystal,' she snapped.

He hooked his binoculars and camera over a broad shoulder and gestured up the lawn. 'Then let's go.'

One of the things Lawson Giordano had got five years ago had been *her*, Cheska thought bitterly, as she tramped beside him. In his bed. Though he had not wanted her, in the lusting, besotted, longing-to-possess-her sense. Far from it. As, just now, he had kissed her for a reason, so he had made love to her then for a cold-blooded, selfish and deliberate reason. Cheska's footsteps quickened. She had forbidden herself from thinking about that long-ago night, and how the touch of his hands, his mouth, his tongue had driven her wild, and she refused to think about it now. It was too demeaning, too embarrassing. Of course, then she had been young and gullible, whereas these days she was mature, alert and——

'Yipes!' Cheska squeaked, as her foot skidded out from under her.

Abruptly finding herself on the verge of performing the splits, she made an instinctive grab for Lawson's arm. He stumbled, swore, and for a moment also seemed about to fall. Then he recovered his balance and held her upright.

'Are you accident-prone?' he demanded, his fingers biting into the flesh of her bare arms, 'or is doing pratfalls every five minutes your way of pepping up a slow day?'

Cheska wrenched herself free. 'I slipped because my flip-flops happen to be wet and muddy,' she informed him frostily.

'Then take the damn things off.' Lawson looked down at the flimsy sandals. 'They were never designed for trekking up hill and down dale anyway.'

She scowled. Forget maturity; he was making her feel like a dim-witted three-year-old.

'I know, but they were at the top of my suitcase and...available,' she said, in ineffectual protest, and, barefoot now and with the flip-flops dangling from her fingers, Cheska set off again beside him over the grass. 'Which product are you promoting this time?' she enquired.

'Product?' Lawson repeated, as if he did not know what she was talking about.

She darted him a glance through the thick veil of her dark lashes. 'It's—it's not a car?'

Five years ago they had met because she had appeared in a commercial which he had been directing. It was her one and only involvement in such a thing, and had come about because, at the time, she had been dating the son of a motor dealer. A millionaire motor dealer who marketed luxury cars and who had decided to boost his sales with an advertisement on television.

'Driven by an upmarket brunette making her way home at dawn after a night of passion with her lover?' Lawson said pithily. He shook his head. 'There won't be a car in sight, I swear. However,' he continued, striding lithely uphill, 'don't be surprised if you wake up one morning next week to find a chorus-line of ten-foot-high fish fingers shimmying their way through the herb garden.'

Cheska's march halted and she gazed at him in horror. Built around 1750, and incorporating an earlier Queen Anne house, Hatchford Manor was a striking Georgian property of elegant proportions, graceful lines and tall windows. It reeked history and, surrounded by wooded acres and lush meadows, occupied an idyllic setting. But to use it as a backdrop for some cheeky, chirpy, vaudeville-type commercial would be sacrilege.

'You're kidding!' she protested.

Lawson slid his hands into the hip pockets of his jeans, an action which contrived to pull the denim tight across his thighs. It was an action which Cheska noticed, though she wished she hadn't.

'Why would I kid?' he enquired.

She started to walk again. He would kid because, for some totally unwarranted reason, he considered her to be a snob and it would amuse him to rattle her.

As though deep in contemplation, Cheska pursed her lips. 'Y'know,' she said, shining a defiant smile, 'on second thoughts, dancing fish fingers sound like fun.'

'Don't they?' Lawson said.

Cheska had hoped to detect a clue as to the validity of his claim, but neither his expression and nor his tone had given anything away. Yet even if he was promoting breaded fish, which had begun to seem more and more unlikely, he would do so with style. Prior to her advertising début, other commercials which he had made had been pointed out to her, and without exception they had been imaginative, well-crafted and by far a cut above the usual. Apparently he had received several awards.

She had not seen anything he had directed since, but it would be surprising if his standards had dropped. Lawson Giordano had cared about his work. Cared passionately.

Though if his standards had plummeted she was not bothered, Cheska decided, as they approached the house. All she wanted was for him to do whatsoever he had come to do and leave. Soonest. A commercial should take no more than three or four days, and for that time she would make certain their paths did not cross again. She had not envisaged spending her first days home holed up in her bedroom or going off for long walks, but if that was what was necessary, so be it.

'Where are you staying?' Cheska enquired, wondering whether he had based himself in Tunbridge Wells, the nearest sizeable town, or had elected for the more homespun comforts of an Olde English country pub.

'Here,' Lawson said.

She shot him a startled glance. 'In the manor?' she protested.

How could she avoid him if he was staying in the same house? Cheska wondered feverishly. Spacious and roomy though Hatchford Manor was, it would be impossible. Her mind buzzed. She would get a girlfriend to invite her to stay next week. She would telephone——

'No, in one of the oast-houses,' he said, and pointed beyond the ivy-covered walls which enclosed the gardens at the rear of the manor to where two conical red-brick towers with white caps topped a timbered brick building.

'They've been newly converted,' Cheska said, as relief at his being under a different roof flooded through her. 'When I left two years ago the building was virtually derelict, but Rupert brought in an architect. Plans were drawn up for a pair of semi-detached houses and, after endless progress reports, he wrote last month to say they were finally finished and ready for habitation.'

'You've been abroad for two years?' Lawson enquired.

'Almost, and I was abroad for a two-year stint prior to that. In the olden days, oast-houses were where the hops used to be dried,' she went on. 'Hops are dried flowers which give a bitter taste to——'

'Beer. You don't need to explain,' he said. 'I went to university in Sussex.'

Cheska cast him a surprised glance. 'I'd realised from your English that you'd probably lived in England at some time, but I had no idea it was in this part of the country. Being a student and then returning to film in the area is quite a coincidence,' she observed.

Lawson looked straight ahead. 'Isn't it?'

Even though he had studied here, for him to have become so fluent and to have lost almost all trace of an accent meant that he must have a natural flair for languages, Cheska reflected, as they walked on. But Lawson Giordano seemed to have a flair for many things—not least lovemaking. Raising her eyes, she watched a pack of black swifts streak across the sky. For years she had obliterated all thoughts of the night they had spent together, and she was not going to resurrect any memories now.

'What's the oast like?' Cheska asked.

'There are stone walls, oak beams and thick white carpets. It comes with all mod cons and is very comfortable. Whoever rents it will be delighted, especially as I believe they're also to be given the use of the manor's swimming pool and tennis court.'

Her brow furrowed. 'The oasts are to be rented out?'

'To holidaymakers.' Lawson swung her a mocking look. 'The prospect of *hoi polloi* setting their grimy feet on her hallowed ground makes my lady shudder?' he enquired.

Cheska's lips thinned. He had misread her bewilderment for snooty objection. Once condemned as toffee-nosed, always condemned, she thought angrily.

'No, but I understood that the oasts were meant to house a couple of gardeners and their families,' she retorted.

'Then you understood wrong.'

Cheska was silent and pensive for a moment. Had Rupert said the oasts were for gardeners or had she assumed it?

'How did your location people discover Hatchford Manor?' she enquired.

'They didn't,' Lawson said. 'It was offered to them.'

Cheska's winged eyebrows soared. Her stepbrother was a scholarly individual whose consuming passion in life was moths and butterflies. As one of the world's leading lepidopterists, Rupert Finch had identified new species and written several books on the subject. But he rarely took an interest in television, and she was astonished that he should have known of the TV companies' requirement for locations; let alone felt inspired to submit his home and his routine to the obtrusion of a film crew.

'Rupert sent in details?' she asked.

'I believe it was Miriam who submitted them.'

'I see,' Cheska said thinly.

Shortly after her departure two years ago, there had been a mention in one of her stepbrother's letters about him renewing his friendship with Miriam Shepherd, a former childhood sweetheart and near-neighbour who had not long been widowed. Miriam was a dreadfully well brought-up, insufferably bright individual who loved to take charge, and while Rupert's increasing references had made it clear that he did not object to the woman being around, Cheska had always found even a small dose of her extremely trying. But having a commercial made at the manor would give Miriam much to talk about at her bridge games and coffee mornings, and, as its instigator, would put her firmly centre-stage.

'You've met Miriam?' Cheska enquired.

Lawson nodded. 'When I came to discuss filming on a couple of earlier occasions and again on my arrival yesterday. She seems to be a constant visitor.'

Cheska uttered a silent scream. From Rupert's letters it had appeared that the woman might be muscling in and attempting to establish herself—which would be easy because her stepbrother was far too malleable—and this was confirmation. Her brow furrowed. Now that she thought about it, it seemed likely that using the oast-houses as holiday homes had been Miriam's idea. The fiftyish blonde had a keen eye for money; which was doubtless one

of the reasons why
at Rupert again, Che

'How old were you w
Rupert's father?' Lawson

'Er... ten,' she said, surpr
subject and surprised that he sh

'How did you get on with your
Cheska smiled. 'Very well, though,
his sixties, he seemed more like a grandf
a father. Desmond Finch was a gentle m
same as Rupert.' Her smile faltered. 'Un
nately he and my mother were only togeth
for——'

'Yoo-hoo,' a voice shrilled, splitting through the
still of the morning, and they both looked up to
see a corseted figure in a vividly floral dress and
pearls flapping a hand from the manor's pillared
porch.

Cheska's heart sank. Miriam Shepherd might be
a constant visitor, but did she have to arrive so
early?

'Yoo-hoo, Lawson!' the woman yodelled.

She shot him a glance. 'Lawson?' she queried
tartly. 'It sounds as if the two of you are friends.'

'The best of,' he said, stopping as they reached
the semi-circle of the metalled forecourt, 'and don't
crinkle your patrician nose like what. Miriam's a
good-hearted type.'

'Good-hearted? Huh! What are you doing?'
Cheska protested, as she was abruptly tipped off
her feet and swung up into his arms.

'Carrying you to the front door.'

She frowned at him. 'Why?'

. 'Because
ne in your
you'll slip.'
had died,'

at bringing
er case, it'll
e no desire
s the most

en thinking
want to be
d not want
d not want

she had decided to set her cap
ka thought scathingly.
hen your mother married
nquired.
ised by the veer in
uld be interested.
tepfather?'
as he was in
ather than
an, the
ortu-
er

to feel the warmth of his hands on her bare legs or the rub of her body against his body as he walked.

'My flip-flops have dried—see?' she said, flourishing them in front of his nose. 'So I shan't slip and you can put me down.'

Lawson shook his head. 'My self-preservation instincts say no.'

'But I say yes!'

'You're in the hands of someone bigger and more powerful than yourself,' he informed her, 'so why not just lie back and enjoy the ride?'

Cheska's temper fizzed. Self-preservation came a low second, she thought darkly, what he was really doing was demonstrating his control over her—in a patronising, condescending, *infuriating* kind of way. And what made it even more infuriating was the sight of gossipy Miriam watching from the porch. Doubtless by this time tomorrow half the population of the county would know how she—

an independent, intelligent young woman—had been toted around like some daffy doll.

'Put me down!' Cheska commanded, in her most majestic tone. 'Twitching your pectorals like this may be doing wonders for your machismo, but——'

'Relax. If you wriggle, you could make me drop you,' Lawson said, and loosened his grip. 'Do you want that?'

Able to recognise a threat when she heard one, Cheska hooked a hasty arm around his neck. Being unceremoniously dumped would be even more demeaning than being carried.

'No, thanks,' she muttered.

'I thought not.' His eyes dipped to the swell of her breasts in the low neckline. 'Besides, carrying you like this is...stimulating.'

'For you, maybe,' Cheska retorted, 'but not for me.'

'No?' Slowly and deliberately, Lawson lowered his gaze again. 'That's odd; all the evidence points to——'

Her cheeks flamed. He had not bothered to finish his sentence, but he did not need to. Belatedly—and to her dismay—she realised that being carried in his arms had aroused her. Her nipples had tightened and, without looking down, Cheska knew they would be jutting like miniature thimbles beneath the black Lycra.

With agile ease, Lawson took the steps up to the porch two at a time, where he set her down on her feet.

'I didn't want my lady to slip,' he told the eagle-eyed Miriam.

Cheska seethed. If he called her 'my lady' once more, she would slap him. She *would*. And never mind Miriam broadcasting the news far and wide.

'Sir Galahad,' the older woman declared, with a simpering smile of admiration. She cocked a curious head. 'Do you two know each other?'

'Intimately,' Lawson replied, hooking his thumbs in the pockets of his jeans and standing with long legs set apart. 'The truth of the matter is——'

Cheska's nerve ends shrieked. He couldn't tell her... He mustn't...

'That he's joking and we met just now, down at the pool,' she gabbled, shooting a daggers-drawn look which defied him to argue.

The last thing she needed was for Miriam to know that something had happened between them—no matter how long ago. An avid ferreter and something of a prude, if the blonde sniffed a whiff of something untoward she would not cease digging until she had unearthed the facts. *All* of them. Cheska shuddered. Her behaviour may have been less than circumspect, but she refused to be branded as a scarlet woman.

'Yes, we did,' Lawson said, being dutifully obedient, though an impudent gleam shone in his dark eyes. 'You were calling me?' he asked Miriam.

'There's a phone call from Mrs Croxley, Janet's mother.' Ushering him indoors, she wafted a beringed hand down the wide, oak-floored hall with its worn Persian rugs, to where a door stood open into the library. 'She promised to hold on.'

'Thank you,' he said, and strode away.

'Francesca, how nice to see you again,' Miriam declared, with a gracious smile. 'Rupert tells me you had a good flight.'

She nodded. 'It was fine. Where is Rupert?' she asked, for her stepbrother was usually an early riser.

'He's getting up. After such a late night last night, he overslept.'

Wondering if she could be being blamed for her plane's midnight arrival time, Cheska shot a suspicious look, but all she saw was raging affability.

'You're probably wondering why I'm here,' Miriam went on. 'Friday's my day for going into Tunbridge to do my weekly shop, so I thought I'd stop by as usual to see if dear Rupie needs anything.'

'That's kind of you,' Cheska said, because it was. Though it could also be regarded as a way of the blonde insinuating herself into 'dear Rupie's' life, she thought astringently.

Miriam smiled. 'My pleasure. While we're alone there's something I feel I must say.' She paused, fingering her pearls, and her tone became that of the clucking mother hen. 'It would be so nice if, this time, while you're home, you could pay for your board and lodging. After all, you are a working girl and you can't expect dear Rupie to finance you for ever.'

Cheska's spine went ramrod-stiff. Her eyes darkened to a stormy grey. She did not consider her dealings with her stepbrother were any of Miriam's business and she resented the interference. The woman might shop for Rupert, but that did not grant her the freedom to meddle in other aspects of his life!

'I don't expect him to finance me,' she replied glacially, then stopped.

She had never paid for her keep. Whenever she had offered, her stepbrother had always refused. There was no need, he had told her, and indeed, until her modelling had made it unnecessary, he had insisted on giving her an over-generous allowance. Cheska's brows drew together. She was perfectly willing to pay, but what did she pay with? Her salary had not been high and, when she had given up her job two days ago, she had also given away all of her savings. Given them away rashly, it now seemed, though she did not regret it.

'So suppose we say thirty pounds a week? That seems fair,' Miriam declared, in a tone which said the matter had been amicably settled. As Lawson reappeared from the library, she swivelled. 'Not trouble, I hope?' she enquired, for as he walked towards them he was frowning.

'I'm afraid so. As you know, we'd arranged that Janet would join me here today, but——'

'She can't?' Miriam rushed in. 'What a shame. Janet's an absolute sweetie,' she informed Cheska. 'She accompanied Mr Giordano—Lawson,' she amended, flashing him a smile, 'on his earlier visits and——' her conversation switched to Lawson again '—I could see how close the two of you were. How you shared an affinity.'

He nodded. 'Unfortunately, last night Janet was rushed into hospital with acute appendicitis,' he continued. 'She's been operated on and——'

'Oh, no!' the blonde broke in again, fluttering a hand to her ample bosom in what, to Cheska, seemed extravagant dismay. 'How dreadful!'

Who was this Janet? she wondered. Lawson's girlfriend? His live-in lover? Perhaps even his wife? The idea brought Cheska up with a start. It had not occurred to her that he might now be married, yet why not? His looks, his intelligence and his sex appeal made Lawson Giordano an undeniable catch and he must be all of thirty-five, an age by which most men had settled down. Her brow puckered. It was irrational, yet the prospect of his having a wife made her feel strangely... piqued.

'How is the poor girl?' Miriam enquired.

'Doing well,' Lawson reported, 'but——'

'Thank heavens!' she crooned, this time stopping him to affect extravagant relief.

'But her convalescence means that Miss Croxley has decided she must withdraw from the shoot,' Lawson completed, a touch impatiently, 'and I need a PA.'

So Janet—*Miss* Croxley—was not his wife, but his personal assistant, Cheska thought. Though this would not exclude her from also being his girlfriend. Indeed, Miriam's reference to and his acknowledgement of their affinity more than hinted that way.

'What kind of duties would an assistant be required to perform?' Miriam enquired.

'She'd have to type up notes, take and make phone calls, help me with the thousand and one matters which need attention during filming.' Lawson massaged his jaw. 'I'll have to contact the office and see if they can rustle someone up and send them down from London, though it's short notice and——'

'Don't bother,' the blonde cut in, smiling. 'I have a replacement.'

'You do?' he said. 'Who?'

Like a magician producing a white rabbit from a top hat, Miriam triumphantly flourished an arm. 'Francesca.'

CHAPTER TWO

CHESKA'S mouth gaped. 'Me?' she protested.

'Thanks, but no, thanks,' Lawson said, simultaneously.

'It's the ideal answer,' Miriam declared, in a voice which sounded as though she was chewing on a bag of marbles. She stopped to listen as noises drifted down the baluster staircase from the first floor. 'Rupert sounds to have finished his shower, so I must see to his toast.'

Cheska felt a spasm of annoyance. Her step-brother's ladyfriend had not only established herself as near enough a fixture, she also appeared to be running the show! Which included taking over the housekeeper's duties.

'Can't Millie do it?' she enquired, an edge to her tone.

'Millicent and her husband are away on holiday for two months, visiting their daughter in Canada,' Miriam informed her. 'Would you care for some toast, too, Francesca?' she continued, being tediously pleasant and well-mannered.

Cheska resisted the urge to tell her, most impolitely, what she could do with the toast. 'No, thanks,' she replied. 'I'll get my own breakfast after I've showered.'

'Then please excuse me,' Miriam said, and click-clacked cheerfully away down the hall on her high heels.

'Having you as my assistant would be anything but ideal,' Lawson said, as the well-upholstered figure disappeared.

'I agree,' Cheska rapped back.

'For a start, the hours are long and antisocial. I often dictate notes in the evening ready for filming the next day, which means I need someone who's good-natured, amenable and everlastingly willing, whatever the time and whatever the strains and stresses.'

Dropping her flip-flops down on the polished wooden floor, she slid her feet into them. As she had already vetoed the idea, there was no need for him to embark on a more detailed job description; though, of course, by stating his requirements, Lawson was also stating what he considered she was *not*. It was yet another dig. Another condemnation. A further chance to indulge in a gratuitous bit of Cheska bashing.

She shone a saccharine smile. 'And I would only work for someone who was understanding, even-tempered and everlastingly considerate,' she retaliated.

His jaw clenched and, for a moment, he seemed about to launch a spirited defence, but instead he chose to ignore her.

'My PA must also be a skilled practitioner of shorthand and typing,' he said.

'I am,' Cheska told him.

Lawson gave a disbelieving laugh. 'Since when?'

'Since I packed in modelling and took a course at secretarial college. For the past four years I've worked as a secretary, so my shorthand and typing speeds are high. I've also manned telephones, fixed trips, dealt with a wide variety of problems and people. In other words, I can do whatever Janet can do.' She shone another saccharine smile. 'Chew on that, *bambino*.'

He frowned. 'Why did you stop modelling?' he enquired. 'As I recall, you were in great demand. You'd appeared on the cover of *Vogue* and——'

'Maybe, and maybe if I'd knuckled down to it I could have reached the top. Who knows?' Cheska's slender shoulders rose and fell. 'But modelling was something I'd been talked into because other people felt it was right for me, not a career which *I'd* chosen.'

The general consensus that modelling was her forte had been because of her looks. In all modesty, Cheska knew she was pretty—the oval face with fine bone-structure and huge grey eyes which she saw in the mirror every morning told her so, likewise the compliments which had been coming her way since she was knee-high. But, all in all, her looks had been something of a liability, and were a sore point right now.

'And having been talked into it, after just a year or so you decided you wanted out. Why?' Lawson asked.

'Because I found standing in front of a camera, mute and striking poses day after day, deadly boring,' Cheska replied, and her chin lifted.

She had given him an ideal opportunity to come back with some crack about her having a short attention-span—in other words, to imply that she was a bimbo—and she was prepared. But, to her surprise, he nodded.

'I've always thought that modelling must be a hell of a strain on any thinking person's sanity,' he said. 'Was boredom the reason why you swanned around?'

Not expecting such acuity, Cheska nodded. 'If anything came along which seemed like it'd be more fun, I went.'

'And you had the means to do so. Life's a bed of roses for some people,' Lawson remarked drily, then, turning his broad wrist, he inspected the steel and gold watch which was strapped to it. 'Someone might be at the office, so I'll ring and see if the wheels can be set in motion for locating a substitute assistant.'

'Before you use the telephone, don't you think it would be polite if you asked permission?' Cheska said, as, having offloaded his camera and binoculars on to the carved hall table, he started to walk away.

She was not in the habit of pulling rank, but, as a stranger in the house, his behaviour seemed just a little too familiar.

Lawson stopped to bow a dutiful head. 'Please, ma'am, may I have your permission to use the telephone?' he recited.

'You may,' she replied stiffly, for his tone and the smile which tugged at the corner of his mouth were mocking.

'Thanks. However, there's really no need for me to ask, not when you consider that, as from yesterday, the production company's been responsible for Hatchford Manor's telephone account.' He strode away. 'And that,' he was tossing the words back at her across his shoulder, 'also as from yesterday, the library's been doing duty as my office.'

Cheska stared at him along the length of the hall. 'Your office?' she said weakly.

'Just until Monday, when phones are being installed in the oasts,' Lawson replied, and vanished.

Cheska sank down on one of the high-backed chairs beside the table. The morning had been a long procession of surprises. One after another they had hit her, until now she was feeling shellshocked and, due to the lack of sleep, also a little weary. Were there any more surprises in store? Please, no. Cheska plucked at the damp edges of her shorts. Not only had Rupert's ladyfriend established herself at Hatchford Manor, but Lawson Giordano appeared to be well entrenched, too. And if she remained here for the next week, there was no way she could escape him. She wanted to remain, Cheska thought wistfully. After so long away, she had been looking forward to renewing her acquaintance with the house which occupied such a fond place in her heart. Besides, why should she feel hounded out?

Stretching out her legs, she frowned down at her feet. Much as it went against the grain to admit it, Miriam's 'ideal answer' would solve one of her problems—for a while. Television companies were known to pay good wages, and if she acted as Lawson's Girl Friday the cash she received would enable her to make two, three or maybe more weekly contributions towards her keep. Her grey eyes became steely. Now that Mrs Busybody had raised the issue, she was determined to pay, even though Rupert would not be fussy. Her pride in-

sisted. And, after all, Cheska acknowledged ruefully, she had been pampered for far too long.

As the murmur of Lawson's baritone sounded
from the library, she wiggled her toes. In order to
keep up the weekly contributions she would need
to find herself a permanent job. Smartish. On the
flight home she had decided that she had had her
fill of both working abroad and of the big-city
hustle-bustle of living in London, and that she
would prefer to work locally. Maybe for a vet, or
a village solicitor, or a farmers' co-operative.
Cheska sighed. Such jobs were thin on the ground
and finding one could take time.

Abruptly she looked up, alerted by the creak of
the floorboards to the fact that Lawson had completed his call.

'Any luck?' she asked.

He shook his head. 'The woman in charge of
personnel had gone in early so I managed to speak
to her, but she reckons there's no chance of finding
anyone who comes within a mile of Janet's
efficiency at such short notice. She says she can
send me a temp or a girl from the typing pool, and
I guess——'

Cheska rose to her feet. 'I'll do it. I'll be your
assistant,' she said. 'I'm efficient, plus——' her jaw
took on a blockbuster slant '—I'm good-natured,
amenable and everlastingly willing, whatever the
strains and stresses.'

'OK, you're hired,' Lawson said.

Her grey eyes widened. She had expected barbed
observations and heavy sarcasm, not straight-
forward acceptance. She had expected to have to

battle. But he must have listened to what she had said and accepted that, in her, he was being given the opportunity to employ a first-rate assistant.

'You've changed your mind?' Cheska enquired, with an arch smile.

'Haven't you? Look, I'm tied to a tight budget,' Lawson said impatiently, 'and if someone comes down from London it means paying for them to stay in a hotel, whereas you——'

Her nostrils pinched. 'Whereas I'm cheap?' she demanded.

'You said it, not me. Cheaper,' he amended, before she could protest. 'How does two hundred pounds a week sound?'

Cheska considered his proposal. She might have offered her services, but she would not be working for Lawson Giordano willingly. On the contrary; she approached the week's employment with strong reservations. As she knew to her cost, the man was a blackguard and, although there was absolutely no risk of her making the same mistake she had made in the past, she reckoned that this entitled her to 'danger money'.

'Three hundred sounds better,' she replied.

He swore. 'Who on earth do you think is funding the film, the Getty family?' he demanded.

'What I think is that it's the tourist season and a week in a hotel'll cost over a hundred pounds, wherever anyone stays,' Cheska told him coolly. 'Not only that, if your assistant works late then a taxi will be needed to ferry her back each night, and another to ferry her here each morning. That means more expense. However, I'm already on the premises, so——'

'Three hundred it is.' His dark eyes narrowed as they focussed on her. 'But you'd better be good.'

'I'm the best,' Cheska assured him.

'I'll bear that in mind,' Lawson said drily, and picking up his camera and binoculars, he hooked them over his shoulder again.

'Rupie, dear!' Miriam bustled out from the kitchen to stand at the foot of the staircase. 'Rupie, dear,' she cooed again, 'breakfast is waiting.'

'Down in a minute,' a muffled voice replied.

As if in anticipation of his arrival, Miriam dabbed at her lacquered champagne-blonde head, then click-clacked her way along the hall towards them. 'Have you agreed terms?' she enquired, clearly having taken it for granted that their protests had been no more than froth and that the merits of her suggestion would be speedily recognised and endorsed.

Lawson nodded. 'It seems I've got myself an assistant *incredibile*,' he said, kissing his fingers in a pronounced mock-Mediterranean style, but, although Cheska replied with a thin smile, his sarcasm went straight over Miriam's head.

'Having a film shot at the manor will be so exciting,' she gushed, then turned to Cheska. 'Did you know that Nicholas Preston is in it?'

She shook her head. 'No.'

'But you're impressed,' demanded Miriam.

'Very.'

Nicholas Preston was a handsome young actor who, Cheska remembered from her last visit home, had had the critics sighing over the eloquence of his Shakespearian roles and whose dynamism in contemporary parts had seemed to earmark him for stardom. Though perhaps he had already become a star? Her time overseas meant she was out of touch with what was happening in the theatre. Out of touch with so many things, she thought pungently—like the *raison d'être* of the oast-houses. However, one thing she did know—Nicholas Preston would not be performing as a front man to any oversized fish fingers.

'I'm surprised he's willing to be in a television commercial,' Cheska remarked, and threw Lawson an oblique look. 'Of *any* kind.'

'A commercial?' Miriam burst into trilling peals of laughter. 'Oh, dear, Francesca, what on earth gave you such a bizarre idea? It's not a commercial which is being made at Hatchford Manor, it's a film for television. An adaptation of one of the classics, a period costume drama.'

Cheska whirled round to Lawson. Here was yet another surprise, though on this occasion she had been tricked, she thought fiercely.

'You direct costume dramas now?' she demanded.

'Among other things—which means you won't see anything shimmying through the herb garden next week,' he said, and placed a fist to his brow. 'Oh, cruel fate.'

Her grey eyes blazed. From them meeting, Lawson Giordano had been having fun at her expense.

'You are a——' Cheska began evilly, then halted, aware of Miriam listening and realising that there were more urgent issues than badmouthing him. 'How long is this film going to take?' she enquired.

'It's scheduled for six weeks,' Lawson said. 'Of course, these things can overrun, though not usually when I'm in charge.'

Cheska's thoughts flew every which way. She had imagined she would be working for him for a mere week, which had been acceptable—just—but instead she was expected to be his assistant for approaching two months! Her stomach cramped. She rebelled against such a timescale—and yet, and yet... Three hundred pounds a week was a goodly sum and, when multiplied by six, a most useful sum. It would mean that, at the end of filming, she would have enough money to update her wardrobe and pay for her keep for another three, perhaps four months, which would enable her to take her time and be selective about her next job, her next employer. And, after what had happened abroad, her next employer would be required to meet certain stringent criteria.

'You don't mind too much about moving out of your room, do you?' Miriam enquired. 'I appreciate that it's——'

'My room?' Cheska said distractedly. She had a lot to think about and the woman was talking double Dutch.

'Didn't Rupert tell you how the whole of the manor has been requisitioned by the film company?'

Cheska's mind ran amok. She had objected to feeling hounded out, but now it seemed that she was actually, physically *being* hounded out! And by whom? Lawson Giordano.

She swung to him. 'The whole of the manor?' she protested, her tone a mix of horror, hostility and dismay.

He nodded. 'As well as using various of the downstairs rooms for filming, it's been arranged that the first floor will accommodate make-up, wardrobe, dressing-rooms and such.'

'So Rupert is coming to stay with me,' Miriam informed her.

Cheska struggled to take everything in. 'But——'

'He'll have his own room,' the older woman went on hastily, as though she had been about to make prurient enquiries into their sleeping arrangements and issue a strict moral lecture, 'and you're going into the other oast-house, next door to Mr Giordano.'

She felt numb. Rupert had not told her anything about this last night. Not a hint. She might have talked at length, but he could have interrupted, Cheska thought rebelliously, then sighed. He would have kept quiet on purpose, in the hope that his garrulous ladyfriend would reveal all. And why? Because he would have known that when she had realised she was to be turfed out of her room, out of the house, she would argue; and the mild-mannered bachelor disliked arguments.

'We never expected you to ring out of the blue and announce that you were returning,' Miriam carried on, 'so we had no idea you'd be around. However, the oast-house is most tasteful. I dealt with the decoration and furnishing, and I know Mr Giordano considers I did a good job. Isn't that right, Lawson?'

'You did an excellent job,' he assured her, with a smile and a courteous bow of his head. 'I reckon you should set up in business as an interior decorator.'

Cheska winced. How smarmy could you get? And as for Miriam having taste—chances were it would be diametrically opposed to hers.

'When am I expected to uproot myself and transfer my belongings?' she enquired.

'Rupert's coming over to my house on Sunday afternoon, so I'd suggest some time before then,' Miriam said, and shone a hopeful smile. 'All right?'

Cheska replied with a brusque bob of her head.

But it was *not* all right. Any of it. The manor having been commandeered, her being virtually frogmarched into the oast-house, but, most of all, Lawson Giordano being in situ. By quitting her job she might have escaped from one farrago, but she had flown straight back into another!

'That'll be Rupert,' Miriam chirruped, as a door closed somewhere upstairs. 'I must brew his Earl Grey.'

'After you've had your breakfast, we'll make a start,' Lawson said, when the stand-in housekeeper had disappeared back to the kitchen.

Cheska blinked. 'Start this morning?'

'There are a couple of items which need to be dealt with, so I'll see you in the library at ten.'

'Ten o'clock?' she echoed.

The affinity-sharing Janet might have intended to join her boss today—and no doubt they would have gone on to share a weekend of high passion— but she had not imagined being roped in for duty quite so soon. Grief, it was less than twelve hours since her plane had touched down and she had still to unpack! Cheska frowned. Should she say she needed time to sort herself out, both physically and mentally? But if she showed any reluctance her new employer might respond by telling her to forget about working for him; and she needed the money.

'Ten a.m. in the library. You want it in sky-writing?' Lawson demanded, when she continued to gaze at him.

Cheska straightened. 'No, thanks.'

He walked to the heavy oak front door which stood open. 'In that case, difficult as it is to tear myself away, *arrivederci*,' he said, and strode out across the porch, down the steps and disappeared.

Cheska took a bite of wheatmeal toast. 'Why did you let Miriam talk you into lending out the manor?' she enquired.

It was three-quarters of an hour later and she was at the table in the high-ceilinged dining-room with Rupert. After compiling an extensive shopping list—Miriam had insisted on buying provisions for her to use in the oast house, too—the do-gooder had driven off into Tunbridge Wells, and they were finally alone.

'She didn't talk me into it,' Rupert demurred. 'I happen to think it's an excellent idea.'

Cheska hissed out an impatient breath. 'Come on, Rupert, you know you don't enjoy having lots of people around. You know how you hate any up-heaval, any disruption.'

'To watch how a film is made will be mind-broadening,' he declared, his narrow face taking on an uncharacteristic stubbornness. 'And the manor isn't being lent out—not for free. The production company are paying a most generous rent. One which, because they're using the premises in total, amounts to several thousands of pounds.'

'Presumably their monopolising the place was Miriam's idea?' she asked.

As he poured himself a second cup of tea, her stepbrother frowned. 'Well . . . yes.'

Had Miriam made the suggestion with the aim of getting Rupert into her home and more firmly into her clutches? Cheska wondered, as she ate her toast. After two years of friendship, did she hope that six weeks together, when she could pamper to his every need and make herself even more indispensable, might push him into a proposal? Tall and slim, with the air of a public school housemaster, the middle-aged bachelor was an attractive man. Over the years, various females had fluttered their eyelashes in his direction, and yet, although he might have had the occasional liaison, he had never taken much real *notice*. But the references in his letters had made it plain that he was noticing the widowed Mrs Shepherd. Cheska sighed. After devoting so many years to looking after her, Rupert deserved to have someone look after him, and she had hoped he might meet someone and fall in love. But why, if he was falling in love, did it have to be with Miriam?

'You're in urgent need of those thousands of pounds?' Cheska enquired.

'Not at all,' Rupert said hastily, 'but——' he stroked a hand over his thinning blond-grey hair '—a little extra is never to be sneezed at.'

'Where are the snuff bottles?' she asked.

Whether it was an association of ideas—sneeze/
snuff—she did not know, but Cheska had abruptly
realised that the shelves in one of the mahogany
cabinets which flanked the fireplace were bare. For
as long as she could remember, there had been
twenty or so antique bottles on display. Made of
coloured glass, some of them were Chinese and extremely rare. They had been collected by Rupert's
mother, Beatrice Finch, a pompous woman, who
had apparently amassed them to impress visitors
rather than for their beauty.

Rupert hesitated, making her wonder if he could
not remember—which would be typical. Unless it
concerned butterflies, he could be amazingly vague.

'They've been put away, like some other bits and
pieces. They were valuable and, as there are going
to be strangers in the house, Miriam and I
thought——' His voice trailed off. 'It's quite an
honour, having Lawson Giordano make a film at
the manor,' Rupert declared. 'His previous three
films were Hollywood productions. Quality productions, mind. The last one hasn't been released in
this country yet, but it's breaking box-office rec-
ords in the States.'

Cheska laughed, and shaking her head. What her
stepbrother knew about the entertainment world
could be written on a postage stamp, and the few
facts he did know were invariably confused.

'You're getting him mixed up with someone else,'
she said. 'Five years ago, Lawson Giordano was
directing TV commercials.'

Rupert's brows soared. 'Fancy that!'

She cast him a look. He had known of her involvement in the car commercial and, at the time,

she would have told him the director's name, but
he had forgotten. Cheska took a sip of coffee. She
could see no point in reminding him now and
neither was she eager to remind herself. It was not
only the night spent with Lawson which she had
erased from her mind, but she preferred to black
out the entire unfortunate episode.

'So,' she continued, 'the likelihood of him
directing major movies in the States——'

'He has,' Rupert insisted.

'OK,' she said placatingly, 'but in that case why
would he suddenly slum it by doing a historical
drama for television?'

'The film he's making here is prestigious,' came
the protest. 'It's to be the highlight of next winter's
programmes and will be sold worldwide.'

'Maybe, but in cinematic terms it's still peanuts.'

Rupert rose to his feet. He knew she did not believe him. 'Miriam brought over an article which
explained how Lawson's talent has enabled him to
climb to the top of his profession in double-quick
time. It's in the drawing-room, I'll find it.' A few
minutes later, he returned to hand her a newspaper.
'There you are. You must excuse me,' Rupert continued, swallowing down the last of his tea. 'I have
an appointment at the dentist's and I don't want
to be late.' He bent to kiss her cheek. 'It's lovely
to see you again, my pet.'

Cheska smiled. 'And you,' she told him.

After she had read the article once, Cheska read
it again. There it was in black and white, confirmation of everything which Rupert had said.
Resting her elbows on the table, she sank her chin
into her hands. Quoted as making movies which

'grabbed, held and moved audiences', Lawson Giordano was now a highly sought-after and successful director. A hot property. But, in that case, why would he bother with——?

A movement of a finger on the ormolu clock on the mantelpiece caught her eye. It was five to ten. Hastily stacking the crockery on a tray, Cheska sped through to the kitchen. She must wash up. If she didn't, Miriam would notice the dirty pots on her return, and be bound to attend to them. The hot water tap was turned on, lemon detergent added to the water. She refused to give her the chance. Firstly, because leaving the washing-up would make it seem as if she had been lazy, and secondly because for Miriam to do it would mean she was establishing herself even further.

Cheska was wiping the last teaspoons, when the doorbell rang. Thrusting the spoons into the drawer, she dried her hands and dashed out into the hall.

'*Ciao*,' Lawson said, when she opened the front door.

She gave a weak smile. 'Hello.'

With a briefcase held in one hand, her boss looked calm and mentally prepared, whereas she was hot-faced and flustered. Cheska pushed back the tousled cinnamon-brown hair which had tumbled over her eyes. At least she had showered and changed, she thought, as she walked beside him to the library. Her shorts had been exchanged for a tailored cream linen skirt, worn with a scarlet silk shirt, while the problematical flipflops had given way to cream leather sandals. There were golden studs in her ears and a strand of gold around her neck. *Plus*, should he have the audacity to ask, she was wearing all the usual items of lingerie!

As they entered the book-lined room, Lawson indicated an electric typewriter which was on a table in front of one of the casement windows.

'Janet left it here in readiness,' he explained. 'Does it suit?'

'Perfectly,' she assured him.

Striding around the dark green leather-topped desk, Lawson opened his briefcase. 'Could you get this printed?' he requested, producing a film. 'Earlier I was checking on how the morning sun hits the house and I need the pictures in order to fix camera angles.'

'How quickly do you want them?'

'As soon as possible.'

Cheska took the film from him. The last time she was home she had noticed that the chemists' in Soper's Corner, the village four miles away, had offered a same-day film printing service.

'They'll be ready by this evening,' she said.

'Thanks.' Lawson eased his long body down into the swivel chair behind the desk. 'I'd also like to have the notes which I made earlier typed up, but as I suspect you could have trouble reading my writing I'd better dictate them.'

Cheska nodded. 'OK.'

He may have annexed the library as his office, but did he have to be so at home? she wondered, watching as he sorted through various pages which had been taken from his briefcase. His denimmed legs were stretched out and he was swinging idly from side to side in the chair. Resentment sparked.

Lawson Giordano looked as though he belonged here!

Raising his head, he fixed her with level brown eyes. 'Are you intending to commit everything I say to memory?' he enquired.

'Sorry?' Cheska said, then flushed as she realised that not only was she standing there with neither notebook or pen, but she had also been staring at him. 'Give me a moment.'

She took a step to the right, then changed her mind and stepped to the left. Where would she locate writing materials? It was such a long time since she had last been here and she didn't have a clue.

'If you open the long drawer in the table, you'll find that Janet also left a supply of stationery,' Lawson informed her, a mite impatiently.

The stationery consisted of neatly arranged stacks of typing paper, copy paper, carbon paper, and every other item that the on-the-ball secretary could possibly need. As Cheska helped herself to a notebook and pencil, she decided that Miss Croxley was just a little *too* perfect. Chances were she had never felt flustered nor had lost her footing in her entire super-efficient life.

Aware of Lawson waiting, Cheska hastily drew up a chair. 'Shoot,' she instructed, sitting down in front of him.

Lawson's dictation was fluent and brisk, though not too brisk. Normally, she would have had no problem keeping up, but this morning Cheska found herself stretched. Was it due to nerves at being dictated to by *him*, or because tiredness had begun to make her feel woolly-headed? Whichever, when he reached the end of what turned out to be six pages of detailed notes, she was relieved. Among her shorthand had been some hastily thrown down squiggles, though she would decipher them when the time came for typing.

'The cast and crew will be staying at the Mayfly,' Lawson said, moving on, 'and——'

'The Mayfly?' Cheska interrupted.

A former coachhouse which, over the years, had been luxuriously extended and become élitist, the Mayfly Hotel sat on the banks of a trout stream some ten miles away. There was a magnificent golf course, every bedroom came with a four-poster, and the meals served in the rosetted restaurant were regularly rhapsodised over in wining and dining columns.

'We've block-booked the place,' he told her.

Wheels turned in her brain. 'So your substitute PA would have stayed there, at a cost of heaven knows how much?' she protested. 'You got a bargain in me!'

'That remains to be seen,' Lawson said grittily. 'But the Mayfly was not of my choosing and isn't cost-effective. It means that around twenty per cent of the budget will go to accommodating sixty or so people for the duration, and I could have put the money to better creative use. However, could you ring the hotel and confirm that all the rooms will be available for occupation as from two p.m. Sunday. I'd also like——' He stopped as the telephone rang beside his elbow. 'Excuse me.'

As he picked it up, Cheska's mouth pinched. Lawson was making himself much *too* much at home.

'The call's probably for Rupert,' she hissed, 'so shouldn't I answer it?'

'Amy, how are you?' Lawson said in greeting, then he covered the mouthpiece with a large hand. 'It's for me,' he informed her.

She gave a plastic smile. It would have to be! As his conversation got under way, it became clear that Amy was an actress who would be appearing in the film. Initially, she appeared to have phoned to ask whether Lawson knew that Nicholas Preston's wife had just given birth to their first child—he didn't— but this could soon be recognised as an excuse and what Amy really wanted to speak about were some worries she had about her role.

As the call lengthened, Cheska rose and went to sit at the table. This seemed a good opportunity to read her shorthand and work out those scribbled outlines. While Lawson spoke calm, encouraging words behind her, she started to check through. Her brow crimped. 'For the runaway scene, angle the camera——' Angle it where? She thought she had fouled up on just the odd word, but the remainder of the sentence seemed to be missing. As Cheska stared down at the page, the shorthand squiggles began to blur. Her lids fell. Her head drooped.

'Ready?' The voice which intruded into her consciousness came from afar. 'Shall we continue?' Lawson said, much nearer this time.

Cheska jerked upright. 'Sorry?'

He was standing alongside, frowning down at her.

'Is Sleeping Beauty hoping to be woken with a kiss?' he taunted.

Circles of pink bloomed on her cheeks. 'No, I——'

'You're some bargain,' Lawson said blisteringly. 'I'm not paying you an inflated salary to nod off whenever you feel like it. I'm paying you to bloody well work!'

Gathering up as much dignity as she could, Cheska got to her feet. 'I'd missed something you'd said and I was trying to decipher it and, because I'm jet lagged, my eyes closed for a millisecond,' she informed him.

As she stalked past to sit stiff-backed in front of the desk, Lawson returned to the swivel chair.

'You had a long-haul flight?' he demanded.

'From Thailand.'

Lawson looked surprised. 'In that case, perhaps you'd prefer to leave everything until tomorrow?' he suggested.

'Not at all. The part I missed in my shorthand was——' She read through her notes and he filled in the spaces. 'Next?' Cheska demanded, being ultra businesslike.

'When you're taking the film to be developed, would you buy a get-well card and arrange for some flowers to be sent to Janet. This is the hospital.'

When he handed her an address, she frowned at it. Janet might be nauseatingly efficient, but she was also a fellow female; another one who was receiving less than fair treatment at the hands of Lawson Giordano.

'Far be it from me to criticise, but wouldn't it demonstrate just a tad of tender concern if you chose the card for your beloved yourself?' Cheska asked tartly.

'Janet is not my beloved,' Lawson replied.

Her brow creased. 'But I thought the two of you were... close?'

'We are. Because she's worked for me off and on for years now, it's got so that we think along the same lines, the same working lines. However, while Miriam may have referred to her as a girl, Janet is near to retirement age. She's a spinster who, away from work, devotes herself to caring for her mother and three Pekinese.'

'Oh.'

'And, for the record,' Lawson continued, 'I don't have a beloved. Moving around as I have been isn't conducive to meaningful relationships.'

'I suppose not,' Cheska muttered, and remembered his phone call. 'Would you also like me to get a birth congratulations card and some flowers for Nicholas Preston's wife?' she enquired.

He nodded. 'Good idea.' He leafed through an address book. 'This is where to send them.' After she had suggested kinds of flowers and checked on how much to spend, Lawson started returning his papers to his briefcase. 'That's it,' he said, 'and don't worry about missing a word or two in your shorthand because I'll soon lick you into shape.'

'It was a lapse which, once I've had a good night's sleep, won't be repeated, so I shan't require any licking,' Cheska said crisply.

His brown eyes trickled languidly over the curves of her body. 'No?' he murmured. 'Pity.'

Sturdily ignoring the innuendo, she went with him as he strode out into the hallway.

'I've been reading about how you've reached the dizzy heights,' Cheska said, 'and I don't understand why you're doing this film.'

'The storyline and the strong dialogue appealed.'

She gave him a sidelong glance. Was it her imagination, or had his answer sounded rehearsed?

'But you must be inundated with gold-plated offers to direct mainstream movies,' Cheska protested. He had set a brisk pace and she was needing to hurry in order to keep up. 'So——'

'I am, but I'm not too struck on Hollywood's falseness and I'm not interested in becoming a celebrity. And,' Lawson added heavily, when she started to protest again, 'after directing three major productions back-to-back, I wanted time to recuperate, to take stock, and it seemed I might accomplish that if I did something less stressful.' He opened the front door and walked outside, leaving her to hover on the threshold. 'Though, of course,' he added, as he started off down the steps, 'I had no idea that fate was going to sabotage everything by producing *you*.'

CHAPTER THREE

HER eyes wary, Cheska watched as the first of the drawing-room radiators was uncoupled, then swung her gaze out through the window to where fifteen tons of hoggin, a mixture of sand and gravel, was being systematically spread over the forecourt. She fidgeted with the belt which cinched the waist of her mocha-coloured shirt dress. Lawson might have claimed that a period drama came low on the cinematic stress scale, but her nerves were stretched as tight as piano-wire—and it was barely noon on Monday.

There were two reasons for her edginess: firstly, her determination to get to grips with her new job as soon as possible; and, secondly, the changes which were taking place in the house. Right now, it was the changes which bothered her the most.

'The radiators need to be handled carefully,' Cheska said, as the two technicians hoisted the ancient bronze-painted unit up into their arms. 'If they were damaged, they'd be virtually impossible to replace.'

'Don't fret, chuck,' one of the men replied, 'we won't let them come to any harm.'

As the radiator was carried out into the hall, Cheska followed, needing to squeeze through a gap between a battery of lighting engineers who were assembling spotlights on one side, and kneeling electricians who were disguising wiring and sockets on the other. She would just take a quick look at how the radiators were to be stored.

'That adhesive tape does come off easily?' Cheska enquired, as she passed an electrician.

'Like a dream,' he assured her.

At eight o'clock that morning, a convoy of vans and buses had drawn up in the cobbled yard to one side of the manor and from them had spilled technicians of multifarious kinds. The dedicated film crew and cast members had followed. Work had begun on doctoring the house, so that the upstairs was functional and the ground floor became the home of a prosperous eighteenth-century squire. As she had jotted down her new boss's instructions—obtain a weather forecast, confirm the date for the extras to arrive, chase up some costumes which had not yet come to hand, *et cetera*—Cheska had attempted to keep track of the alterations, though with intermittent success. But now Lawson was holed up with some of the cast for a rehearsal, and she had been released prior to lunch. And now much of the furniture had been banished to the outhouses and replaced, there were new carpets, and suits of shining armour stood to attention in the hall.

Cheska hastened after the radiators. While she had not expected Rupert to oversee the transformation—it would never occur to him—she was surprised that Miriam had not taken it upon herself to supervise. Contrarily, she had hoped she would. Efficient though the workmen might be, she considered that someone should watch over, chaperon, offer the occasional pertinent reminder. But, after appearing mid-morning and being introduced to the

actors, Miriam and Rupert had driven off to find
a pub lunch.

At an ear-splitting thwack-thwack-thwack,
Cheska abandoned the radiator and swerved
towards the dining-room. The noise was a staple
gun, an implement she had quickly learned to dread
and, on entering, she saw that the faded green velvet
curtains had been removed and a false pair in rich
ruby brocade were being stapled into their place.

'Careful!' she cried, sprinting forward.

The pony-tailed youth who was firing the gun
stopped to mutter something beneath his breath. 'I
am being careful. I've pinned a million things and
never caused any damage,' he bit out, sounding as
though, given a chance, the millionth and one item
he would choose to staple would be her mouth.

Cheska peered past him at the window. 'Even so,
I really do think that——'

'It's my lunchtime,' he declared, and flung down
the gun.

'Finish the curtains, Wayne,' a voice instructed.

Turning, she saw Lawson standing in the door-
way. Clad in a black open-throated shirt and black
Levis, he looked saturnine, stern and annoyed. Had
Amy Kennett made a shambles of the rehearsal?
Cheska wondered. Ever since her arrival the ac-
tress, who was a fragile-looking girl with cropped
Titian hair, had been reiterating the anxieties which
she had voiced on the phone.

'Yes, sir,' the youth said obediently, and picked
up the gun. There was a long rattle of noise, and
the ruby-red drapes were in place. 'OK if I take a
break now?' he asked, with a grin.

Lawson nodded. 'Go ahead.' He waited until the youth had disappeared, then strode forward. 'I'd be obliged if you wouldn't continually hassle everyone,' he rasped.

'I'm not,' Cheska protested.

'All morning you've been darting off to bombard ears with unnecessary advice,' he said. 'You've been obstructing and impeding.'

Her eyes widened in surprise. It wasn't Amy Kennett he was mad at, it was her! She frowned. Had she really fussed that much?

'I didn't mean to be a nuisance,' Cheska said. 'It's just that—well, I never realised the alterations to the house would be quite so drastic.'

'Historical accuracy is crucial,' Lawson said. 'It's useless us doing the damn story unless we keep faith.'

'Granted, but even though you're making a film here, this does happen to be my home and so naturally I'm keen to ensure that——'

'You're a part owner of Hatchford Manor?' he cut in sharply.

Cheska shook her head. 'No, but my ownership isn't the point. The point is that Wayne tends to be cavalier with the stapling gun and I don't want holes to be left in the window frames.'

'In woodworm-eaten frames where another few hundred holes or so would go unnoticed,' Lawson said, striding across to examine the window. He slid his hands into the pockets of his jeans and came back to her. 'Nor do you want the already badly scratched floorboards to be scratched. Or rugs which are virtually falling apart to be untidily rolled.'

She gave him a turn-to-stone stare. How dared he walk in and find fault? All right, so he had leased the house for a period, but that did not allow him the right to criticise.

'Hatchford Manor may be elegantly faded,' Cheska said, in icy tones, 'but——'

'Hatchford Manor is downright shabby! And don't just stand there baring your teeth at me.' Clasping her shoulders in two large hands, Lawson turned her around. 'Look!' he instructed.

Cheska looked and her brow furrowed. She had not noticed it before—probably because she was so used to it—but everything did seem shabby. Dilapidated, almost. When had the inside of the house last been decorated, or the outside painted, or any repairs done to furniture and fittings? She thought hard and realised it could not have been for years. Several years. Her stepbrother might have transformed the oasts, but he had done nothing here.

'So Rupert needs to get his act together,' Cheska said, stepping away so that Lawson had to release her.

Like most Latins he was a tactile man, yet while, to him, his hands on her shoulders would be a negligent gesture, she found it . . . disturbing.

'What it needs,' Lawson told her sternly, 'is for specialist craftsmen to examine the property in detail, decide what should be done, and bring it up to standard. It'll be a lengthy operation and it'll cost, but Hatchford Manor is a beautiful house which deserves and demands sympathetic restoration. It's part of the heritage of this country, and to allow it to fall into disrepair and crumble would be a sin.' A golden-skinned hand sliced down the air in an impassioned gesture. 'A *crime*.'

Cheska's spine stiffened. While she agreed with him, she objected to what amounted to a condemnation of her stepbrother's stewardship.

'If Rupert has neglected his responsibilities, it's only because he's absent-minded,' she declared.

Lawson arched a thick black brow. 'Is that so?'

'It is,' Cheska snapped and, annoyed because he appeared to be insinuating that Rupert's neglect had sprung from some other, more sinister reason—like he had deliberately not bothered—she moved from the defensive on to an irritated attack. 'But what makes you care so much about Hatchford Manor?' she demanded. 'How come this country's heritage is of such deep concern to you?'

'It concerns him because fifty per cent of the thick red blood which flows through his veins happens to be English,' a languid voice pronounced, and Nicholas Preston strolled into the room.

Blessed with aristocratic good looks and a slim, elegant build, the actor seemed a little too conscious of himself and his appearance. His corn-gold hair was slicked trendily back from his brow and his astonishingly blue eyes—forget-me-not blue, so his fans drooled—were identically matched by the colour of his long-sleeved shirt. Tight-fitting moleskin trousers flattered his hips. Clearly Nicholas Preston had not thrown on the first clothes which he had found in the drawer that morning.

Cheska flashed him a quick smile, then looked at Lawson. Although she had assumed him to be thoroughbred Italian, she had wondered how he had acquired his first name.

'Your mother is English?' she asked.

'She was.'

'She's dead?'

A barricade seemed to build in his eyes, holding her off. 'She died a long time ago,' he replied, and turned to Nicholas. 'How's Portia and your daughter?'

'Portia's fine, but——' the new father looked disgusted '—the kid woke up at two o'clock last night and again at four, and bawled blue murder.'

'I hate to break this to you, but babies have a tendency to do that,' Lawson remarked drily.

'Especially when they're so tiny,' Cheska added.

'Then thank goodness I'll be away from it for most of the next six weeks,' Nicholas declared.

A head appeared around the door. 'Lawson, can you spare a minute?' a lighting engineer asked. 'We've fixed the spots, but before we split for lunch perhaps you'd check that they meet requirements.'

'I'll be with you,' he promised, but first he took another look at the windows. 'You could be right about Wayne,' he said. 'I'll ask him to ease up on the staples.'

Cheska smiled. 'Thank you,' she said.

If he asked, Wayne *would* ease up, she thought, as he departed. While Lawson possessed a natural authority which commanded respect, his employees also liked him and did their best to please him. He might have become a man of clout in the film world, but he had no edge and already he had established the mood on the set, which was one of everyone being equally involved and pulling together.

'That looks like a quaint picture-postcard village,' Nicholas remarked, strolling over to point out to a huddle of pan-tiled houses on the brow of a distant hill.

'It is. It's Soper's Corner. The settlement was mentioned in the Domesday Book and many of the buildings are——'

Cheska was launching happily into a potted history of the village when the actor cut in.

'Fancy joining me for a bite to eat?' he suggested.

She hesitated. Although a canteen wagon was dispensing food in the cobbled yard to one side of the manor, she had intended to go back to the oast-house and make herself a sandwich.

'It'd be an opportunity for us to get to know each other,' Nicholas went on, with the lift of a blond brow and an appealing smile.

Deciding that their establishing a rapport could only be beneficial for her job, Cheska nodded. 'I'd like that,' she said.

When they went out into the hall, it was empty. The lighting men, the electricians, and Lawson, had gone. Tilting her head to one side, Cheska listened. The whole house was silent. After a morning of non-stop activity, everyone must have departed for lunch.

'Not that way,' Nicholas said, when she turned towards the front door. He clasped her elbow. 'In my dressing-room. I ordered a hamper from the hotel and they've provided far too much.'

'Why don't we picnic on the lawn?' she suggested, as her escort ushered her up the stairs. 'It's a lovely day and there're lots of people out there and——'

'Not enough time. In half an hour I must get changed into my tight white breeches——' he slung her a sideways look, as if expecting her to fall in a swoon '—ready for this afternoon.'

Leading the way along the wide landing, Nicholas turned into a room which, until that morning, had been one of the guest bedrooms. Now the carved wooden bed was pushed against one wall and a modern tan leather sofa and two armchairs incongruously occupied the space in the centre. In the bay window was a round dining table, with a large wicker hamper set on top. After closing the door, the actor became busy setting out delicacies such as smoked salmon, cooked king prawns and individual dishes of various *hors d'oeuvres*. Next came place settings of Willow Pattern china, silver cutlery and heavy white damask napkins. Finally he produced a bottle of expensive German wine. The Mayfly was living up to its *cordon bleu* reputation today, Cheska thought wryly.

Her host waved a magnanimous hand, 'Help yourself,' he said.

As he uncorked the wine, she took slices of avocado and smoked salmon, and a serving of green salad. A crusty poppy-seed sprinkled bread roll was buttered.

'Not for me,' Cheska said, when Nicholas had filled one crystal goblet to the brim and was about to pour another. 'I'd prefer fresh orange juice.'

He gave a little-boy pout. 'But, honey——'

Removing a carton from the hamper, she flipped the cap. 'If I'm to do my job properly, I need to keep a clear head.'

'You're far too delectable to be working behind the camera,' Nicholas advised her solemnly, when he had sampled his wine. 'You should be in front of it. You should be an actress.'

'No, thanks,' Cheska said.

He seemed to have expected his statement to send her into a delighted tizzy, but she had had her go at acting in the car commercial, and once was enough. More than enough.

'But you're such a stunning looker. You knock the spots of old Amy, and with that stupendous shape and those legs——'

Her host's low whistle was followed by him moving into what seemed like automatic overdrive with a practised charm and chat. He told her how he had immediately noticed her, how drawn he had felt, and although he did not quite say, 'Where have you been all my life?' he came close. Cheska sipped her orange juice. She had visualised 'getting to know each other' to mean a general camaraderie, but from his you-and-me smiles and conversation it was clear that Nicholas had a far more physical alliance in mind. It could not be by chance that the hotel had provided so much food and *two* place settings, she reflected, and if she had turned down the Romeo's invitation he would, it seemed, have promptly corralled some other girl.

'You only have to give me the nod and I'll speak to all the right people,' Nicholas declared, bringing his chatting-up to an end with a further insistence that she was tailor-made for stardom. He placed a hand over hers and squeezed it tight. 'I've never offered to do that for anyone else before, but for you——' the forget-me-not blue eyes glued themselves to hers '—anything.'

Cheska extracted her hand and surreptitiously inched her chair away. 'No, thanks,' she said, a second time.

'Now, honey,' he started to purr.

Should she walk out? She wanted to, but hesitated to offend him. Her relationship with the film's director was fraught enough, without turning the principal actor into an enemy. Cheska moved her chair further away, noticeably this time, and lifted her knife and fork. For a minute or two she ate alone, but then Nicholas sulkily cracked open a prawn. Their meal proceeded in silence.

'Lawson told me he was doing this film because he needed a chance to recuperate,' Cheska said, when her plate was empty. 'Do you think he was telling the truth?'

Her companion gave an offhand shrug. 'Why not? If the studios were eating out of my hand there's no way you'd find me disappearing into the backwoods, but the guy's not big on glory. He reckons that what he enjoys about his success is the power it's given him to choose, and I guess that meant he could choose to film at Hatchford Manor.'

'Did he know this was to be the location?' Cheska enquired.

'I believe that's part of what attracted him. More smoked salmon?' Nicholas offered, a touch moodily.

'No thanks.'

'Crème brûlée?'

'Please.'

'Lawson won't be being paid a fraction of what he could get,' the actor continued, as he worked his way through the prawns, 'but it's not as though he needs the cash. The deals he's had on his last three productions gave him a percentage of the profits and as the first two've grossed millions he must be raking in the readies like crazy. Add what's still to come in from the third film and you're talking serious money.'

Cheska ate a spoonful of her dessert. It must be laden with calories, but it was delicious.

'Weren't the powers that be being ambitious when they approached him to do a historical drama for television?' she asked.

'He wasn't approached,' Nicholas said. 'By chance, he happened to hear on the grapevine that the original director had been forced to drop out due to production delays and——' an abortive attempt was made to snap greasy fingers '—what do y'know, he promptly offers to take over. The bosses couldn't believe their luck and neither can I. To have the chance to work with someone of his stature, even if it is only for the box, is——' There was a knock at the door. 'Come in,' he said, and the subject of their conversation strode into the room.

With his expression sombre and his shoulders squared, Lawson looked like someone on the alert for trouble—and well able to deal with it.

'I noticed the two of you were missing and it struck me that you could be together,' he said, his gaze spearing straight at Cheska before moving coolly on to her companion.

'Just having a spot of lunch,' Nicholas declared boisterously.

'An expensive spot,' Lawson remarked, with a glance at the laden table. 'Still, if you wish to run up a hefty personal account at the Mayfly that's your choice.'

A stain of colour rose up the younger man's neck. 'A personal account?' he asked awkwardly.

'There *are* those who attempt to sneak extras into their expenses in the hope that the accountants won't notice,' Lawson said, strolling forward to tear the corner off a slice of smoked salmon and put it into his mouth. He chewed for a moment. 'But you know how important it is that we keep within the budget, so you won't do that.'

Nicholas's colour deepened. 'Good grief, of course not!' he exclaimed, but his simulation of shock would have won him no Oscars.

In the somewhat tense silence which followed, Cheska pushed back her chair and got to her feet. 'Thank you for lunch,' she said, giving her host a polite smile, 'but it's time I returned to work.'

'It's time we all returned to work,' Lawson remarked, with a pertinent look in Nicholas's direction, and accompanied her out of the room. Together, they made their way along the landing. 'What you get up to in your lunch break is nothing to do with me,' he said.

'Correct,' Cheska put in, before he could proceed any further.

By being caught alone with Nicholas and eating his food, she had felt guilty of committing some kind of misdeed. Or, to be accurate, that was how

Lawson had made her feel, and it nettled her. She had done nothing wrong.

'*Unless,*' he went on heavily, 'it interferes with the production of this film, and you fraternising with Nicholas could do.'

'I was not fraternising!' she retorted, for the derisive curl of his lip had made his meaning brutally explicit.

'So I interrupted things.'

'There was nothing to interrupt,' Cheska rapped back. 'Nicholas may have had certain ideas, but I wasn't interested.'

Lawson gave a terse laugh. 'Then why agree to a private tête-à-tête?'

'When I accepted his invitation I thought we'd be eating outside at the canteen wagon like everyone else, and when I accompanied him to his dressing-room I wasn't aware what he had in mind.' She did not add, 'So there!' but it was implied.

'Lay off it,' he derided, 'Nicholas is famous for his hyperactive libido. It's less than a year since his antics on another set made headlines in the papers, and you'd have to have worn a paper bag over your head not to have seen them.'

'Or been living in Thailand,' Cheska said succinctly.

They had reached the head of the staircase, and here Lawson stopped. 'True,' he acknowledged. Leaning back against the wide wooden banister, he pleated his lower lip with thoughtful fingers. 'So you didn't join Nicholas——'

'In order to fraternise? *No.* What kind of a person do you think I am?' she demanded. 'I wouldn't get involved with a married man.' Cheska paused, a shadow crossing her face, and then continued with some heat, 'I knew Nicholas was married, I knew his wife had just given birth to their first child, and yet you have the nerve to accuse me of rushing up to his dressing-room within hours of meeting him and fooling around.' Her grey eyes spat sparks. 'How dare you?'

Lawson raised a hand. 'Calm down,' he said. 'I made a mistake and I apologise.'

'Family life is important to me,' Cheska said, her anger gathering momentum and carrying her on. 'It's sacred, and I would never, ever, enter into a situation where I might cause pain to someone's wife, to their children. I would never wreck a marriage and I object to your——' she was spluttering out the words '—your slander.'

'There's no need to look at me as though I'm something low down on the evolutionary scale,' Lawson protested. 'I've said I'm sorry.'

'So you should be!' She continued to glare at him for ten, twenty, thirty seconds, then marched off ahead down the stairs. Had she overreacted and protested too much? Cheska wondered. Maybe, but extramarital affairs were a touchy subject. 'What did Nicholas get up to on the other set?' she enquired in a calmer voice, when Lawson came alongside a few moments later.

'He was having high jinks with an actress and Portia got wind of it. Much as she loves the guy and intends to hang on to him, she doesn't trust Il Cutie Pie one inch so wherever he works she makes sure she has a spy. Portia used to be a continuity girl and has contacts throughout the industry,' he explained.

'Does she have a spy here?'

'I understand the wardrobe mistress is a buddy. A year ago, after receiving a phone call one day, Portia stormed on to the set and into Nick's dressing-room,' Lawson continued, 'where she found him and the actress *in flagrante delicto*. Not only did she proceed to give him merry hell, but she went after his *amour* with a vicious left hook.'

Cheska gave a startled laugh. 'She actually hit her?'

'And cracked a tooth. Portia is a feisty lady, but then,' he said, giving her a dry look, 'there's more than one of them around. However, someone blabbed to the Press, who had a field day. After that Nicholas became surly, the actress was like a cat on a hot tin roof, and the film turned out to be a shadow of what could've been. So give our leading man a wide berth in future,' Lawson instructed. As they stepped off the last stair, his voice became steely. 'You haven't exactly laid out the red carpet for this film, but there's no way I'll let you louse things up a second time.'

'I didn't louse things up before,' Cheska protested, with vehemence, then lowered her voice. Lunchtime was nearing an end and people had begun to drift back indoors. An electrician had gone into the drawing-room and a couple of women were walking in through the front door. 'I never saw the car commercial, but everyone who did said it was excellent,' she hissed.

'And why was it excellent? Because I made it so. However, if you'd had your way,' he said, his fury rising to the surface even five years on, 'it would've been——'

'You were obsessed by that commercial,' Cheska denounced, attacking back.

'Like hell! All I——' Lawson stopped. 'We mustn't fight. It's going to be hot under the lights when we start filming and the cast will need something to drink, so I was wondering if you could drive into the village and pick up some mineral water?' His lips stretched into a slow captivating smile. 'Please?'

Bemused, Cheska looked at him. A moment ago he had been armoured with hostility, but now the brown eyes had softened and Lawson's tone was gentle.

'Water?' she repeated.

Placing an arm around her shoulders, he shepherded her along the hall. 'The catering folk were supposed to have brought supplies, but they didn't. And it shouldn't take you many minutes. You can use my car if you like.'

Cheska thought of the gleaming silver Mercedes coupé which he had parked in one of the garages. His offer was generous, but she had never driven such a powerful or expensive vehicle before, and suppose she had a bump?

'Thanks, but I'll stick to mine. I'll go straight away,' she told him.

'Thanks.' His hand moved up to touch the silkiness of a cinnamon-brown curl. 'Your hair's longer than it was before,' Lawson murmured. 'It suits you.'

Feeling stupidly and unreasonably pleased, Cheska smiled. 'Thank you.'

His dark head was bent to hers and, as the faint fragrance of his sandalwood aftershave filled her nostrils, her heartbeat quickened. When she had spent the night with him she had been held in that captivation and thrall which some people called love, and she knew why. With his incisiveness, his confidence, his virility, Lawson had made an *impact* on her emotions. It had been an impact which no man had ever made before, and one which she had been unable to ignore.

'How much water shall I get?' Cheska enquired. 'A dozen of those big plastic bottles, if the shop has them in stock?'

'Please.' As they walked through the door and out on to the porch, Lawson removed his arm from her shoulders. 'That should've done it,' he said.

'Done what?' she asked.

'Fooled Portia's contact. You saw the women who went past us and up the stairs?'

Cheska remembered seeing them enter the house and knew they must have gone by, but she had been so busy looking at him she had not noticed.

'Um—yes.'

'The taller of the two is the wardrobe mistress, and if she'd realised that you and Nicholas had gone missing over lunch and was suspicious, she won't be now.'

She stared. 'You mean you were being...friendly on purpose?'

'While I'd like us to be friends, my main priority is ensuring that the film proceeds without any unnecessary hiccups,' Lawson said, and grinned. 'Pitiless bastard, aren't I?'

Cheska's hands clenched into fists. He had not only fooled the wardrobe mistress, he had fooled

her, too—and she had sworn he would never get
the better of her again!

'I'd like you back with the water and ready for
us starting filming at two o'clock,' Lawson continued, becoming serious. 'Think you can manage
that?'

Snapping to attention, Cheska gave a furious
salute. 'Yessir!' she declared, and marched off.

As she climbed back into her ancient Volkswagen,
Cheska looked at her watch. Although the general
stores had had the required supply of mineral water,
it had been in a lock-up at the back and the boy
who had been sent to bring the bottles had taken
ages. Now the time was ten minutes to two. Still,
she should just make it. Accelerating swiftly into
top gear, she drove along the high street, out of the
village and down the hill. Cheska sighed. In be-
guiling her, Lawson had been unscrupulously
tapping into the sexual attraction he knew she still
felt for him. Her fingers tightened around the
steering wheel. Why was she so responsive? Why,
when she knew the kind of man he was, had she
allowed herself to be bewitched, to be controlled?
It defied all rational analysis.

As she rounded a corner, her foot slammed down
hard on the brake pedal and the Beetle juddered to
a halt. Ahead, filling the narrow lane from hedge
to hedge, and ambling towards her, was a herd of
cows. A large herd, which stretched back as far as
she could see. Cheska cut the engine. Unless she
returned to the village and took a lengthy detour,
this was the only road to the manor, so all she could
do was wait. And wait. And wait. In what seemed

like studied slow motion, the cows lumbered by, together with a couple of prancing dogs, a youth who winked at her, and, after an age and bringing up the rear, the elderly farmer.

'If it's not Cheska,' he said, stopping to lean on his stick and cast a gap-toothed grin in through the window. 'Didn't realise you were home, my lovely. Had a good time in—where was it—Taiwan?'

'Thailand,' she said. 'Yes, thanks.'

'I'll tell the missus I've seen you. Not been well for months, the missus,' he said dolefully. 'Just after Easter she took a nasty dose of the flu and ever since——'

As the farmer embarked on a long rambling tale of woe, Cheska dutifully commiserated. She was itching to get away, but the poor man seemed desperate to talk and cutting him short would have been unkind. The minutes ticked by, and the last of the herd were long gone by the time his recital came to an end and she was able to decently tell him goodbye.

'Give my regards to your wife,' Cheska said, hastily gunning the engine. 'I'll call in and see her some time.'

'She'd like that,' the farmer replied, but the Volkswagen had already shot away.

As Cheska drove across the floor of the valley and up the hill on the other side, she had another look at her watch. It was twenty past two. Damnation. A punctual return had been important. Not only had she said she would be back on time, but, after claiming to be the epitome of efficiency, she was eager to prove it. This far, everything Lawson had asked her to do had been accomplished with swift aplomb—though because she was new to the job it had not been easy—and she had wanted to keep it that way. Cheska frowned. An added spur had been the fact that one of the things she could remember him complaining about at the time of the commercial had been her tardiness.

At a painted sign marked 'Hatchford Manor', Cheska swung off the lane and on to the winding unmade drive which led steeply up between thickets of trees. She would only be half an hour late at most, she thought, as she bounced in and out of potholes, and, with luck, Lawson would be too preoccupied to notice.

As she approached the opening on to the yard, once again she skidded to a halt. Inside on the cobbles, the victualling wagon and other film-related vehicles were neatly parked, but slewed across the entrance at an angle which completely blocked her entry was a yellow telecommunications van. An unoccupied van. Cheska groaned. The phones were being installed in the oasts today, so the engineers would be somewhere around. Pressing her hand on the horn, she blasted out a please-move staccato. She waited. The oasts were beyond the yard, behind the manor, and she felt sure that the men must hear, whether they were working inside or out, but no one arrived. She thumped on the horn again, and waited again. To no avail. Climbing out of the car, Cheska unloaded the heavy tray of water. She would deliver it, then go round to the oasts and rout out the engineers.

The bottles clutched against her chest, Cheska was making her way laboriously across the yard,

when a tall figure appeared from around the front
of the manor.

'I'm buying a gun,' Lawson said, as he strode
forwards.

'I beg your pardon?'

'What do you think you're playing at?' he demanded, planting himself in front of her.

A sense of danger prickled her nerve ends.
Although his voice had been quiet, it was deeply
angry and she detected an undercurrent of violence
in the tautness of his body. He had noticed she was
late and he was furious—though this seemed
extreme. Cheska tightened her grip on the water.
Surely the cast were not actually *dying* of thirst?

'I'm sorry, but I couldn't help it,' she said.

'You couldn't help sounding your horn?'

Cheska looked blank. 'My horn?'

'It was you just now, blasting out a couple of
boogie-on-down choruses of "Rally Round the
Flag, Boys"?'

His leaden sarcasm unsettled her. 'Er...yes.'

'I knew it,' Lawson said scathingly. 'I knew it'd
have to be you who made the noise which was
picked up on the sound and ruined the take. The
fifth take. The only decent take!'

'But I never thought——' Cheska began.

'Never thought, or just didn't give a damn?'
There was an acrid twist to his mouth. 'I'd settle
for the latter.'

'That's not fair,' she protested, but he took no
notice.

'You know what appealed to me about you?
What I thought was your vulnerable streak. But
you're as vulnerable as a commando. Boy, you

really saw me coming, didn't you?' Lawson stormed on, the yellow flecks starting to blaze in his eyes. 'Though why you ever agreed to act as my assistant, my *helper*, God only knows, when you seem intent on wrecking this production, just as you were intent on wrecking the commercial.'

Cheska felt a rip-roaring burst of adrenalin. 'Baloney!' she shot back.

'Five years ago, you didn't go all out to hinder?' he demanded.

'*No.*' Abruptly, she hesitated. 'I may not have been falling over myself to take part in the thing, but I never——'

'You not only have an amazing capacity for ignoring the facts,' Lawson cut in damningly, 'but you've obviously done some creative rewriting and editing of the past.'

Cheska looked at him. His dark head was thrown back with the Roman nose proudly angled, and he was waving his arms around in strong, dramatic gestures. While she objected to being maligned, she could not help thinking that his anger was rather splendid... and strangely exciting.

'It was only a commercial,' she said.

'*Only* a commercial?' His voice roughened, thickened, curdled. 'So it didn't matter that you were a complete and utter pain in the ass?'

Cheska heaved up the water. If anyone had rewritten the past, it was him. But she did not want to become involved in a discussion about it and have mud thrown at her now.

'I agreed to work for you because a girl must eat,' she said, in a placatory voice, 'and——'

'You're scratching around for the next crust?' he cut in, his eyes flicking scornfully over her beautifully cut, silk dress. 'Perhaps you shouldn't spend so much on designer clothes.'

Cheska bit down a retort. The dress was at least eight years old, a relic from the days when she had been the recipient of Rupert's largesse.

'And I don't want to wreck anything,' she continued determinedly. 'Sounding my horn was a genuine error because I'm new to filming and didn't realise it could be picked up on the sound. I've apologised——' she shone an appeasing smile '—so there's no need to put me through the wringer.'

'That wasn't the wringer, that was a light rinse; the heavy duty cycle comes next,' Lawson informed her, squeezing the words out in a hiss.

As she chafed against his anger, Cheska's own temper began to burn. He might be someone who, when bitten, bit back, but need he bite with such ferocity?

'You mean there's no chance you'll listen to reason and I'm still to be scolded? In that case, you can hold this,' she said, and pushed the weighty tray of bottles at him.

Her thrust was impetuous and her aim erratic. As the package rammed up hard against his thighs, Lawson grabbed hold of it, bent and swore.

'You're attempting to neuter me?' he demanded, as he straightened.

'I didn't succeed?' Cheska enquired caustically. 'Remind me to bring my castration kit along with me next time.'

Lawson took a firmer grip on the water. 'Let's get one thing straight,' he rasped. 'There's no way I'll be subjected to six weeks of mental anguish.'

'And there's no way I'll be barked at for the next six weeks!' she retaliated.

'Then perhaps we should call it a day.'

'Call—call it a day?' Cheska faltered.

'The locations company have similar properties to Hatchford Manor on their books, so——' Lawson's eyes narrowed into lethal slits '—all I need to do is pick up the phone and the shoot can be switched to somewhere else.'

Cheska gazed frigidly back. If he insisted on believing she was some kind of unguided missile running around, that was his problem.

'So switch it,' she declared, flicking a curl of burnished brown hair back from her shoulder. 'I can think of nothing which would give me greater delight.'

CHAPTER FOUR

SOMEWHERE from behind Cheska heard a gasp and
Miriam hurtled forward, her high heels clattering
over the cobbles.

'You can't take the film away,' she protested, in
a dismayed, panic-stricken falsetto.

Cheska looked at the woman in astonishment.
Where had she come from? Then her gaze lifted,
stretched, circled, and she saw that not only had
Miriam been standing with Rupert and two telephone engineers who had arrived from the oast-
houses, but, on the other side of the yard, hovered
a cluster of cast and crew who must have trailed
their boss from the manor. All were looking on.
The equally astonished looks which Lawson was
giving their audience indicated that a public
dressing-down had not been on his agenda, but that
was what had happened. Cheska's cheeks began to
burn. They had been providing a burlesque act?
Lord, how humiliating. If only a hole would appear
in the ground and swallow her up.

Lawson frowned at Miriam. 'I can do whatever
I consider is appropriate,' he informed her curtly.

The protester gave a strained laugh. 'But—but
think of the preparatory work which has already
been done, of the upset to all these good people,
of the time which'll be wasted. I don't know what
the problem is, but I do know that problems can
be overcome.' An eagerly soothing hand was placed

on his arm. 'Always. So why don't you continue filming, while I have a little talk with Francesca?' she suggested, in the benevolent buttery tones of a mediator.

When Lawson switched his frown from Miriam to her, Cheska's chin lifted. Was he about to launch a fresh attack? If so, she was ready, and never mind the onlookers. However, after subjecting her to a long, immobile stare which seemed to challenge her to speculate on what was going on in his mind, her opponent abruptly swivelled and, with the bottles of water in his arms, strode back towards the manor.

As he passed by, his minions swung round *en masse* and dutifully followed. Watching them, Cheska decided that there was no way *she* would ever dutifully follow him around again. Indeed, she had just resigned from her job! Miriam may be anxious to smooth things over—the premature withdrawal of the film would mean a loss of face with her cronies—but she refused to kowtow. Lawson Giordano might have censured her in the past and censured her today—both times for scant reason—but he would not be allowed another opportunity.

'Rupie dear, could you be a poppet and move the car?' Miriam called, indicating the Volkswagen which was preventing the departure of the telephone engineers. 'Francesca and I are going to take a walk in the garden.'

'Straight away,' Rupert said obligingly.

That task organised, the older woman lost no time in ushering Cheska through a gate in the yard's perimeter wall and into the section of the walled gardens which was dedicated to roses. Planted several generations ago, the huge cabbage and climbing roses filled the air with their heady perfume.

'Now, Francesca,' Miriam said, her manner that of an officious yet fair-minded headmistress, 'what was the reason for the contretemps?'

'I sounded my car horn and ruined a take.'

'Oh, dear.' There was some tut-tutting, then her companion frowned. 'That was all?'

It was not all, Cheska thought. Much of Lawson's fury had been inspired by their history, but she did not feel inclined to take a revealing trip down Memory Lane for Miriam's benefit.

She nodded. 'I sounded the horn without thinking and I said I was sorry, but——'

'You must tell Mr Giordano that you're sorry again.'

Cheska shook her head. 'No.'

'You *must*,' Miriam insisted, and shone a balm-pouring smile. 'His temper may have become a little frayed, but directing a film means the poor man's carrying all kinds of unimaginable burdens, so——'

'The "poor man's" temper was more than a little frayed,' she cut in pithily. 'It was wrath-of-God time.'

'He's a creative person, and those who're creative tend to be a touch temperamental.'

'He was downright bolshie!' Cheska protested.

'But Mr Giordano is Italian,' the older woman declared, fastening on to yet another excuse, 'and Italians are emotional people.'

'Lawson is half English,' she replied, 'though whatever his ancestry it doesn't eliminate the fact that the man's a tyrant.'

'I haven't noticed him acting like a tyrant before,' Miriam demurred.

'Perhaps not, but he acts like one with me!'

'I wonder if Mr Giordano's being part English is why he reminds me of Rupert,' Miriam said, all of a sudden, as they walked along the red brick path which cut between the rose beds.

Cheska gave a hoot of protesting laughter. 'They're nothing like. Their colouring is completely different, dark as against fair, but also Lawson is far more forceful, decisive—and argumentative,' she added grimly.

'Even so, there's something about the way he walks, the way he holds his head which has a definite echo of Rupie,' Miriam declared. She indicated that they should sit on a wrought-iron bench in the sunshine. 'We can't have Mr Giordano leaving,' she said, returning to her original theme.

Cheska cast her companion a glance. She did not appear to be blaming her for the upset, but, whether or not she was, she refused to feel guilty. She had done all she could to make amends and if, at the end, she had told her antagonist good riddance— well, like everyone else's, her patience had its limits. She sighed. Though trading verbal punches in stand-up fights had never been her style. It was only Lawson who seemed capable of rousing her to such heights of annoyance—as he had once roused her to similarly fevered heights of desire.

'If he goes, it's his choice,' Cheska said. 'I'm sorry your arrangement has come to an unexpected

end and it's unfortunate that the house has been
turned upside down for nothing——'

'But if Mr Giordano goes, so does the rent,'
Miriam protested.

Cheska frowned. The older woman was always
so ferociously cheerful, yet within her protest she
had heard a note of real and naked distress. The
rent was the root cause of her panic, she realised,
not any possible embarrassment with her friends.

'The money's important?' Cheska enquired, re-
membering her stepbrother's assertion to the
contrary.

Miriam flushed, twisting her pearls. 'Well——'

'It is,' she said, as, all of a sudden, everything
slotted into place.

Now Cheska understood why the oasts were to
be holiday homes, why the manor had been offered
to the location company, why the property was in
such poor condition. And why she had been asked
to contribute towards her board and lodging.
Although Rupert had deliberately misled her, it
seemed so obvious that she was amazed it had not
occurred to her before, and, she realised, there had
been other clues.

'Rupert's sold the snuff bottles to raise cash,'
Cheska said, recalling his hesitation when she had
asked about them. Her mind went to other items
which she had noticed were missing from their usual
places. 'And the grandfather clock...and the gilt
console tables...and——'

'The silver George the First communion cups,'
Miriam said. 'He had no option. Over the past few
years, share prices have fallen and the value of the
portfolio which his father left him has dwindled.

Dear Rupie's never been interested in either acquiring money, or spending it, and so——' her expression was both regretful and fond '—he hasn't properly kept track. He simply took a regular income from his investments and told his accountant not to bother him. However, four or five years ago, the man demanded a meeting and warned that he was skating on thin financial ice.'

'Rupert's been short of cash all that time?' Cheska protested.

'I'm afraid so.'

'Then how could he afford to renovate the oasts?'

'With the aid of government grants,' Miriam told her. 'But now he's having to search for every penny he can get, which is why you must apologise to Mr Giordano. You'll do that?' she implored.

Cheska sighed. All her instincts rebelled against going to him and *grovelling*—which he would doubtless expect—but as her stepbrother had had no option but to sell off some of his possessions, she could see no other option open to *her* now.

'Of course, I will,' she agreed.

'Thank you, thank you, thank you,' Miriam said, burbling in her relief. 'Please don't mention his money troubles to Rupie. He prefers you not to know about——' She stopped abruptly, to look up and give a shamefaced smile. Rupert was walking towards them along the path. 'Oh, there you are, dear. Francesca's happy to apologise to Mr Giordano, so everything's going to be all right. It was a storm in a teacup.'

Rupert sat down beside Cheska. 'Thanks,' he said.

'You're welcome,' she replied, giving his arm an affectionate hug.

He looked across her to his ladyfriend. 'Were you telling Cheska how I'm in dire straits?' he enquired.

Miriam's plump cheeks reddened. 'Um...' she said uncomfortably.

'It's all right,' Rupert said. 'I've decided that I'd better come clean. Cheska's a smart girl and, no matter how much I dissemble, how many white lies I tell, she's bound to realise sooner or later.'

'She has realised,' Cheska told him.

Her stepbrother gave a rueful smile. 'In that case, I'll put you properly in the picture,' he said, and embarked on an account of his financial situation. 'So you see,' he completed, some time later, 'although there're still several more items which can be sold, my regular income has almost dried up.'

'You should have told me all this before,' she protested.

Rupert examined the pattern on his tie. 'Maybe, but—well, you've had more than enough to cope with in your life and I didn't want to saddle you with my troubles.'

'The things I had to cope with happened when I was a child,' she said, in gentle reproof. 'But I'm an adult now and you don't have to protect me any more.'

'I know, but I suppose that once I'd fallen into the habit I——' He shrugged.

'What we need to do is formulate a plan of action for raising money,' Cheska said, with a look at both her companions, 'which, as Rupert has the house and the land at his disposal, could be in a variety of ways. Then, once his cash-flow has been restored, he'll be able to make a start on repairing the property.'

Rupert glanced across her again to Miriam. 'Repairing the property?' he repeated.

'You must have noticed how the manor is in urgent need of attention,' Cheska protested.

'Well, of course, but——' He glanced at his ladyfriend again.

'First things first,' Miriam said, and rose briskly to her feet, 'which means you making your peace with Mr Giordano.'

As Cheska heard the muffled, yet recognisable, sound of a door being unlocked, opened and then closed, she stiffened. At long last, Lawson had returned to his oast.

Having decided to steer clear of him for the rest of the afternoon—she might be neglecting her duties, but she refused to risk being publicly berated again—Cheska had attended to his outstanding instructions and then driven into Tunbridge Wells. On one of the spa town's hilly streets, she had registered with a secretarial agency. There were no suitable positions currently on their books, but they would, so the smiling manageress had informed her, be in touch. Arriving back late afternoon, Cheska had listened for sounds from the house next door, though fruitlessly, and as the afternoon had faded into evening and her listening had continued she had gradually become more and more wound up. An omelette had been made for dinner, though she had barely tasted it, and now she was sitting at the desk in the sitting-room. On the desk was the typewriter which had been brought over from the library, and for the past hour, and with ear permanently cocked, she had been concocting a list of ways in which Rupert could make money.

But now Lawson was home, and now the time had arrived when she must go, clad in metaphorical sackcloth and ashes, and beg his forgiveness. Cheska frowned out through the latticed window at a sunset painted with glorious hues of pink and gold. And no matter what he might say, however much he might rile her, she must stay calm and subdued and be meekly subservient. Act like a regular wimp. Curses.

Rising, she tweaked at the skirt of her coffee-coloured dress. Both Rupert and Miriam had taken it for granted that the director would accept her apology and stay, but suppose he declared that he was switching the location of the shoot regardless? When Lawson had stridden back into the manor it had seemed as if he would resume filming, but instead he could have put his cast and crew to work on reversing the morning's doctoring in readiness for shipping out. Her gaze swung to the carriage clock on the mantelpiece. Maybe that explained why he had not returned to his abode until almost nine o'clock.

Cheska chewed at her lip. If Lawson had organised a switch, what did she do? Fall at his feet, weep copious tears over his sneakers and beg him to reconsider? Engage him in a reasoned and reasonable explanation of the benefits of remaining? Or, if all else failed, don her shorts and low-cut top and attempt to seduce him? She smiled wryly. He would not have kissed her unless she held some appeal, but that did not mean he was open to seduction. Anything but. Lawson Giordano called the sexual tune, he did not dance to it.

A sudden knock had Cheska spinning round. The oasts had internal access to each other in the form of double doors, one pair in the sitting-room and another upstairs on the landing. This had been at the architect's suggestion so that if, at some time in the future, it was felt desirable for the two houses to be combined into one, it would be easier to do. Each door was fitted with a latch and bolts, top and bottom. Cheska stared. She had kept her door bolted, but Lawson had knocked on it, so he must have opened his.

But why had he knocked? Cheska wondered, in alarm. What did he intend to say? For him to want to speak to her so immediately on his return seemed a bad omen. When there was a second knock, she leapt forward and, with her heart pounding in her chest, drew back the bolts.

'Y-yes?' Cheska faltered, opening the door to find him standing, tall and broad shouldered, before her.

'I want to apologise,' Lawson said.

Her grey eyes became huge. 'Apologise?' she said breathlessly.

'For accusing you of deliberate negligence when you sounded your horn. It was an easy mistake to make, but it happened at a moment when I was ... fraught, and all I can say is——' he spread supplicatory hands '—I'm sorry.'

Not sure whether to burst into peals of delirious laughter, or weep for the unnecessary torture he had put her through, Cheska gazed at him. She did not

have to act the wimp, to be subservient, to grovel—
thank goodness.

'So you won't be moving the film away from
Hatchford Manor?' she said, needing to make
certain.

'No.' Lawson stood to one side, allowing her
access into his house. 'How about joining me for
a glass of wine?' he suggested.

Cheska grinned. Her relief was so profound that
at that moment she would have agreed to almost
anything. 'Thank you.'

As she crossed through the double doors, she
took a hasty look around. With a stone inglenook
fireplace opposite French windows which opened
on to a patio, and a large window on the outer wall,
the layout of the sitting-room was a mirror-image
of next door, though, while her sofa, chairs and
curtains were in shades of russet, tangerine and old
gold, here they were in differing tints of green. Both
colour schemes fitted in well with the white carpet
and country-style ambiance.

'Why were you fraught?' Cheska enquired, when
she was sitting on the overstuffed sofa with a glass
of white wine in her hand.

'Because I haven't directed anything historical
before and so I'm nervous about it.'

'You—nervous?' she protested.

'Very, and because of Amy.' Lawson paused.
'Though I do confess to having a hot temper
and——' his brown eyes tangled with hers '—hot
blood.'

Cheska sipped from her glass. She did not need
any reminder of his hot blood—or her response to
it. Although she had been doing her utmost to

ignore them, memories of the night they had spent together seemed to be increasingly battering at her mind.

'And what did Amy do?' she enquired, her tone carefully conversational and matter-of-fact.

'It was what she *wasn't* doing,' Lawson replied, sitting in the other corner of the sofa. 'She wasn't becoming her character. Until now she's appeared in contemporary roles and she was too slick, too modern,' he explained. 'She'd been worried about it herself.'

'Which is why she telephoned you on Friday?'

'And a hundred times prior to that,' he said wearily, and took a mouthful of wine. 'I told her that once she changed into her costume everything else would change and her character'd fall into place. I half believed it would, but it only needed one take for me to realise that we were in deep trouble.'

'You said the fifth take was decent,' Cheska recalled.

'Decent as in acceptable, though barely.' He rested the foot of one leg on the denimmed knee of the other. 'When we resumed it took Amy damn near all afternoon to manage a second decent performance, and then, many takes later, she was OK with the next few lines of dialogue, and so on. But if she continues at this rate, she's going to push the production way over schedule; and the guys in the grey suits won't sanction that.'

'So what do you intend to do?'

Lawson sighed. 'What can I do but keep on encouraging the girl and pray her performance will jell? However, that's why I lost my cool, and that's why I wanted to apologise for bawling you out over the horn.'

Cheska took another mouthful of wine. His apology was sweet—so far as it went.

'Aren't you also going to apologise for bawling me out over my "hindering" during the commercial?' she enquired, inserting the word between crisp inverted commas.

He shook his head. 'No.'

She bridled. 'And suppose I said that that wasn't good enough?'

'I'd say it's as good as it gets,' Lawson replied.

Cheska's mouth thinned. She had been all set to bury the hatchet, but now she wanted to bury it in his neck! She counted from one to ten. Slowly. No matter how annoying he was nor how irritated she might feel, she could not afford to cross swords with him again.

'You were wise to stay away from me this afternoon,' Lawson continued, and arched a sardonic brow. 'If you hadn't, there was a danger I might have strangled you.'

'You could have tried,' Cheska said pertly. 'Did anything arise which you'd like me to attend to?' she went on, using the query as a reminder that she was still his personal assistant.

'No, and I shan't be making any notes this evening, either.' Stretching long arms above his head, he yawned. 'After all I've had to cope with today——' she received a look '—exhaustion's setting in.'

'Then could I borrow a copy of the script?' she asked. 'I'd like to read it and now seems the ideal time.'

'Sure,' Lawson said, and nodded towards books, files and scripts which were on a table below the window. 'There's a spare one which you can keep.'

'Thanks.' Following his gaze, Cheska saw that the table was made from the base of an old treadle sewing machine which had been topped with a sheet of white marble. 'I recognise that sewing machine,' she said, in surprise. 'For as long as I can remember it's been in a spare room at the manor. Nobody ever used it and it was thick with rust, but now——' Now the treadle had been scraped clean and painted a matt black. She gave a delighted smile. 'It makes a great table.'

'It was Miriam's idea.'

Cheska's gaze travelled more leisurely around the room. As in her oast, the furniture consisted of pieces which had been selected from the manor's ragbag assortment, cleaned and polished, and which fitted in to perfection.

'I misjudged Miriam,' she said ruefully. 'But you were right, she has done an excellent job here.'

Lawson nodded. 'However incessantly effervescent she may be, the woman can put together a mean house. On the stairs she's hung watercolours of hop-picking scenes which——'

At first, as he enthused about the paintings which enlivened the wall of the stone spiral staircase, Cheska listened, but in time her attention strayed from what Lawson was saying to how he looked. She studied him along the length of the sofa. He had thick, black and outrageously long eyelashes— lashes to kill for. His hair, which was thick and black, too, curled behind his ear and covered his head in healthy, glossy, sculpted waves down to his shirt collar. It was the kind of hair which begged to have fingers run through.

'So, if you'd like to, I could take you round now,' Lawson completed.

Cheska blinked. His final sentences had passed her by.

'Sorry?'

'Miriam showed me through your house when I first arrived,' he said, 'but perhaps you'd like to look around here?'

Gulping down the remnants of her wine, she rose to her feet. 'Please,' she said.

With one large and one smaller bedroom, and an olde-worlde-style bathroom between them, the upstairs of Lawson's oast was again a mirror image of hers. But once again the colour scheme was different. Whereas her emperor-size brass bed was covered in a lemon broderie anglaise duvet which matched the filmy lemon on white flowered curtains, his cover and curtains were in a chic fir green. As Cheska admired the charm of the low-ceilinged room, she noticed a bottle of men's cologne on the dressing-table, a shirt hung behind the door, a pair of navy silk boxer shorts left on a chair. Her nerves twanged. All of a sudden she was aware of being alone with Lawson in his bedroom. Alone with him on the entire estate, she realised, for by now the actors and crew would have returned to the Mayfly, and Rupert was several miles away at Miriam's.

'I seem to have misjudged Miriam all along the line,' Cheska declared, suddenly desperate to get past her guide and out of the room, yet wary of making too rushed an exit. 'I thought she might have been attracted by Rupert's wealth, but the truth is that Rupert doesn't——'

Her words dried. She had needed to talk in order to obliterate an edgy awareness of their surroundings and their solitude, yet, in talking, she had galloped to the tactless brink of revealing her stepbrother's shaky finances.

'The truth is that Rupert's near to broke,' Lawson said.

Cheska shot him a startled look. His statement had held the undeniable ring of certainty.

'He—he told you?' she stammered.

Dropping down on the edge of the bed, Lawson patted the space beside him. 'Sit down.'

Cheska stood motionless. She had been planning to make an exit from the room, not join him on the duvet!

'I shan't bite,' he said.

'I didn't think you would,' she replied quickly, too quickly.

As she perched beside him, as stiff as a statue, Lawson's mouth stretched into a slow grin.

'You don't intend to slither all over me?' he enquired, with an amused sideways look.

Cheska's stomach muscles clenched. By reminding her of the last time they had been together on a bed, he was playing calculated games with her tension. Was that why he had brought her up here, simply to frazzle her nerves? she wondered, her distrust of him once again in full bloom. She frowned. Lawson seemed intent on making her pay for what he judged to be her recalcitrance of the past, though she had not really hindered— had she?

Cheska shone a smile as sweet as cyanide. 'Not on this occasion,' she said, recognising that in letting him sense her nervousness she had made a glaring strategic blunder.

'But you enjoyed it,' Lawson murmured. 'You took great pleasure in dragging the tips of your——'

She felt herself grow hot and bothered. 'That happened five years ago,' she interrupted sharply.

'So it did. Sorry,' he said, not sounding the least bit so. 'I don't know why, but you bring out the devil in me. Rupert didn't tell me he was near to broke,' Lawson continued, his amusement fading as he returned to their earlier conversation, 'though he's come close a couple of times and I get the impression that he'd like to. But if you give any thought to the situation here, it's obvious he's living on a shoestring. I was surprised when you didn't seem to have realised.'

'I didn't realise because Rupert had chosen to keep me deliberately in the dark—until this afternoon. But I've already thought of some ways in which he can raise funds and refurbish the manor, and over the next few days I shall think of more.'

'Ways such as?'

'Turning the drawing-room into a café and selling cream teas. Or advertising the use of the swimming pool and tennis courts, for a fee. Or running regular car boot sales.'

'Rupert could also apply to have Hatchford Manor become a listed building,' Lawson said, 'which may——'

'A listed building?' Cheska queried.

There were several in the area, but she was uncertain what being 'listed' actually meant.

'At present there are around half a million in England, falling into three main categories,' he told her. 'Six thousand or so are Grade I, which means they're of exceptional architectural or historical interest. Almost eighteen thousand are Grade II, which covers buildings of particular quality and character, and Hatchford Manor would probably fall into this category. If not, most buildings built between 1700 and 1840 are also listed, though inspectors from the Historic Buildings and Monuments Commission have to survey the property and then select it according to various criteria.'

'You seem very well informed,' she remarked.

Lawson nodded brusquely. 'Once the manor has been approved,' he continued, 'Rupert may be able to apply for a grant to help preserve it, though grants are usually given on condition that the restored property is open to the public, for some part of the year.' He paused. 'He may not fancy opening the house, as he may not fancy marketing cream teas *et cetera*. But, all this is based on the assumption that Rupert wants to remain here. Perhaps he doesn't. Perhaps it's occurred to him that he can solve his money difficulties at a stroke by simply selling the manor.'

Cheska gave a startled laugh. 'Rupert would never do that!' she protested.

'Why not?'

Her rejection had been knee-jerk, coming from a blind rooted conviction, and now she needed to think. 'Because he didn't mention selling earlier and because Hatchford Manor has always been his home.'

'Not always,' Lawson said. 'His mother persuaded his father to buy it, because she fancied herself as the châtelaine of a manor, when Rupert was two or three.'

'All right, for most of his life it's been his home,' Cheska adjusted, then frowned. She was surprised her stepbrother should have spoken about his mother. Their relationship had not been easy and it was rare that he mentioned Beatrice Finch, even to her. 'Rupert told you about his mother wanting the house?' she enquired.

Lawson rose from the bed. 'He could have done, or perhaps it was someone in the village,' he said, shrugging. 'I can't remember. But what I'm saying,' he continued, as he shepherded her out of the door and across the tiny landing, 'is that Rupert might decide to sell.'

'Never,' Cheska said, going ahead of him down the stairs.

'You don't think he'll marry Miriam?'

'I don't know, but he obviously hasn't proposed yet.'

'He'll need to. I can't imagine her being willing to live in sin, no matter how delightful other people may find it,' Lawson said drily. 'And if they marry, they could choose to live in her house. Only this morning, Rupert was saying how pleasant it is.'

Cheska walked through the pine fitted kitchen and back into his sitting-room. 'Maybe, but he wouldn't consider selling Hatchford Manor,' she declared.

'Ask him.'

'I will,' she replied. 'Thanks for the drink. I'll go now and let you get your dinner.' As she reached the doorway, Cheska turned to give him a dry look. 'I take it you are capable of feeding yourself.'

'That's a very patronising remark,' he said, and arched a brow. 'Unless, of course, you're offering to cook for me.'

'I'm not,' she said crisply.

'Then it's just as well my father taught me how to rustle up the odd bowl of spaghetti. But aren't you forgetting something?' Lawson enquired.

For a moment, her mind was a blank. 'Oh, the script.'

'No,' he said, walking towards her, 'the kiss.'

Her pulses tremored. 'Kiss?' Cheska queried.

'You know the saying "kiss and make up"?' Leaning a broad shoulder against the door-jamb, Lawson bent over her. 'We've done the making-up part, so——?'

His brown eyes were gleaming and his mouth was dangerously close to her mouth. Yet again, he was teasing her, undermining her composure, controlling her. Rebellion surged. Right, mister, Cheska thought, two can play at this game.

'Funny you should mention it,' she said. 'I was just thinking the same thing myself.'

Lawson straightened a little. 'You were?' he said, his eyes suddenly watchful.

Reaching up, she touched his cheek, and felt the rasp of stubble beneath her fingertips. She had noticed how, by the end of the day, the golden skin of his jaw invariably developed a faint but darkening shadow.

'I was,' Cheska purred.

His look became wary. 'What are you doing?' Lawson demanded, when she slid her fingers slowly up across his cheek and into the thickness of his hair.

'You have to ask?' she said, smiling.

'I guess not,' he replied tersely.

Cheska drew his head down to hers. 'You only have to say if you think you're out of your depth,' she murmured.

As he looked back at her, there was a moment when his eyes held something indecipherable. 'I'm an excellent swimmer,' Lawson replied.

'In that case, stand by for deep water!' she said defiantly, and pressed her mouth to his.

Whether she parted her lips or whether he parted them for her, afterwards Cheska could not remember. All she could remember was his tongue in her mouth like an invasive force, her breasts pressed against his chest, and, as his arms came around her and he drew her closer into his body, a sudden spiralling heat. Raising a hand, Lawson covered the round up-tilted curve of her breast and as his thumb brushed across the tightness of her nipple, excitement streaked through her. Panic followed on its heels. A galloping panic. Dear heaven, what was happening? What had she started? Cheska wondered. She might be proving that she was capable of giving as good as she got, but she had never expected to be this aroused—so foolishly, confusedly and dangerously aroused. Yet when Lawson abruptly ended the embrace and stepped back to frown, something akin to disappointment stabbed through her.

'You wanted the script,' he said, crossing to get it and tersely hand it to her.

'Thanks.' Cheska flashed a giddy smile. 'I've never read a screenplay before, so I'm interested to do so. And to then see how you perceive the story and focus on the subject matter, and how the cast interpret the words, will be fascinating. It'll be a learning experience,' Cheska declared, and stopped, hearing herself talking like a newspaper. 'Goodnight.'

'Goodnight,' Lawson replied, in a clipped voice.

Almost hurling herself through the door, Cheska shot the bolts and dropped limply down on the sofa. She put a hand to her mouth. Her lips were tingling and the nerves in her body had gone askew. It was unfortunate that she had been so affected by the kiss, but Lawson had been affected, too. His abrupt retreat and brusque manner had indicated his fury at her taking charge. She had rattled him, and so, she decided, consoling herself with the thought, her counter-attack had worked.

CHAPTER FIVE

HATCHFORD MANOR'S upper floor had been given the all-clear and now Cheska was making her way around the ground floor, inspecting each room in turn. It was Friday evening, and before locking up she was checking that windows were fastened, taps had not been left to run, no cigarette ends were dangerously smouldering. After three weeks when the sun had obligingly shone, when Amy Kennett's acting *had* suddenly jelled, when the production was actually running ahead of schedule, Lawson had awarded everyone for their efforts by giving them not just one day off at the weekend, but two. So now the crew and cast had departed and the house was destined to stand empty until eight o'clock on Monday morning. Cheska frowned out through the library's casement windows at the orange ball of the setting sun. Unless, of course, Rupert suddenly decided to sell, contacted an estate agent, and they appeared with prospective buyers.

When she had floated the notion of him disposing of the property, the bachelor had shocked her by admitting that it could be an option.

'But you love the house,' she had protested.

'But if I can't afford it,' Rupert had replied, and smiled. 'Perhaps I'll find I can, once I've considered your list of schemes.'

Cheska sighed. All she could do now was wait and see—and try not to get wound up in the process.

She had been wound up about seeing Lawson again the morning after she had kissed him, Cheska reflected as, having satisfied herself that the room was secure, she closed the library door. In the clear objective light of the next day, her counter-attack had seemed not to have worked so much as to have recklessly exposed her to all manner of reprisals. How would Lawson retaliate—with mocking remarks, with caresses which would sear into her senses, with a further more intimate embrace? His annoyance at her taking the initiative by kissing him was bound to be punished in some way. But which way, and when? On pins when she had joined him, as the day had progressed Cheska had recognised that he was not in the business of retaliation. Not in the business of anything but filmmaking. Lawson had slotted himself into the work mode and, overnight, metamorphosed from being her sexual tormentor into strictly an employer. And, for the past three weeks, he had been the understanding, even-tempered and undeviatingly platonic boss. Alleluia.

Cheska started to check through the drawing-room, the final room. For her part, she had been the good-natured, amenable and everlastingly willing personal assistant, she mused. When taking dictation in the evenings, her shorthand had kept pace, enabling her to present him with accurate and perfectly typed copies of his notes and any correspondence the following day. Her handling of his requests and instructions had been impeccable and, halfway down the track, she felt she was shaping up to be as efficient an assistant as Janet.

At the sound of the front door opening, Cheska tilted her head. This would be Lawson. After seeming to have a firm grip on her role, today Amy Kennett had suddenly hit problems, so he had taken the girl over to the privacy of his oast to talk them through. But now he had returned to close up the manor with her, as he so often did. Cheska smiled. Lawson seemed to enjoy walking round, absorbing the feel of the place and listening to any anecdotes she may have about the Finch family; and she enjoyed it, too. Her smile grew. Now that they operated purely on a work footing, they were getting along well together.

'I'm here,' she called, as footsteps padded along the hall, but when a man walked into the room a moment later it was Nicholas Preston. 'Good evening,' she said pleasantly, yet formally.

Although, since their lunch together, he had made no further approaches, Cheska remained on her guard. An irrepressible philanderer, the actor had spent the last three weeks advancing on just about every other young female in sight, who, doubtless in deference to his wife's boxing prowess, had to a girl rebuffed him. Unfortunately, this had in no way dampened Nicholas's ardour for the chase and, having found her here alone, she wondered if he might once again chase her.

'You thought I was our big noise director,' Nicholas declared.

'I did,' Cheska acknowledged.

'And you're disappointed. You are,' he insisted, before she had time to construct some evasive reply. 'The fall of your face was a dead giveaway.' Spreading his hands on the hips of pristine white slacks, he leaned towards her. 'But, of course, you're hooked on the guy.'

She gave him a startled look. 'Excuse me?'

His handsome features took on a leering aspect. 'You have the hots,' Nicholas declared.

Cheska scrutinised a window catch. Because he felt peeved by her lack of interest, the actor's puffed-up idea of his irresistibility obviously demanded that he find an excuse. And, at random, he had fastened on Lawson.

'You have an over-active imagination,' she told him coolly.

Nicholas made a rude noise. 'Honey, I have eyes and I can recognise evidence when I see it.' As Cheska moved on from one window to the next, he followed her. 'But here's a word of warning from your old uncle Nick—women are Lawson's playthings and film his passion. So if it's commitment you're after, you've picked the wrong guy.'

Cheska turned to give him an old-fashioned look. It seemed pretty rich for the Casanova *par excellence* to be offering such advice.

'You remember I said that you ought to be an actress?' Nicholas carried on. 'I really think you should.'

She groaned. He was still attempting to flatter, still making a play? He might consider himself God's gift to women, but did he never give up?

'I'm not interested in acting,' Cheska replied, her voice edged with impatience.

'But you're very photogenic. I know you're photogenic. I've seen the video,' Nicholas said, 'and——'

'Video?' she interrupted. 'What video?'

'Of a car commercial. I called in on Lawson just now to clear something with him and he was showing it to Amy.' At his mention of the actress, Nicholas turned down his mouth. 'I couldn't believe it when we started our big love scene this afternoon and the silly cow screwed up.' Derisive forget-me-not blue eyes were raised to the ceiling. 'And since then it's been one useless take after another. Frankly, the chance to take a break from Miss Cardboard is a godsend, even if I am doomed to having my sleep wrecked. I'd forgotten my jacket,' he explained, abruptly swinging back towards the door. 'I'll go and get it.'

As the actor disappeared upstairs, Cheska's brows drew together. She had not known Lawson had had a copy of the car commercial, at least, not here. Though she supposed he would keep videos of all his work back at the apartment he had told her he rented in Hampstead. She checked another window. But why had he been showing it to the actress?

'Finished?' Nicholas enquired, reappearing with a navy blue blazer slung around his shoulders in a suave and theatrically casual manner.

Cheska nodded. She set the burglar alarm, locked the front door and went with him round to the yard, where a taxi was waiting. She had ordered it to ferry Nicholas and Amy up to London and their respective homes, but the redhead was nowhere in sight. After another grumble about the sleep he expected to lose, the actor said goodbye and climbed inside.

'If you see Amy, tell her to get a move on,' he instructed, speaking out of the window. 'I don't intend to sit here twiddling my thumbs for much longer.'

'Will do,' Cheska replied, thinking that his thumb-twiddling had lasted for less than thirty seconds.

She had got halfway along the path which led across the rear of the manor and around to the oasts when an elfin creature clad in black from head to toe sprinted around the corner. Cheska grinned. Amy Kennett was a lively if somewhat highly strung individual, and she liked her.

'Have a good weekend,' she said.

'And—and you,' Amy panted, stopping briefly as she reached her. 'Though as you'll be here with your Numero Uno, what else could it be?'

'Sorry?'

'See you on Monday,' the actress said, and galloped off.

Cheska stared at the retreating figure. Why, all of a sudden, were people implying that she carried some kind of a torch for Lawson when, so far as they knew, he was and always ever had been just her boss? When her attitude towards him was simply that of an employee? It did not make sense. Brushing her hair back from the shoulders of the pink skinny-rib top which she wore with faded jeans, Cheska frowned. For him to give a viewing of the car commercial made no sense, either. As she approached her oast, her footsteps swerved. Lawson might have said he had nothing which demanded her attention this evening, but she disagreed.

'Something up?' he asked, when he opened his front door in answer to her ring.

He had a glass of gin and tonic in his hand, and a network of fine lines around his eyes. One of those rare beasts, a creative individual *and* a man of action, Lawson had spent the past three weeks working fourteen hours a day. And, Cheska suspected, had devoted several of the remaining ten to intensive film-orientated thinking.

'Nicholas tells me he's been watching the car commercial,' she said.

'He would,' he remarked drily.

'I'd like to see it, too,' Cheska told him.

When the advertisement had been originally aired, she had steered clear of television. At that time, her emotions had been too tender and too volatile for her to face the memories which would have been so starkly revived.

Lawson frowned. 'It's only a commercial,' he began.

'Only?' she enquired, with the lift of a brow.

'Point taken,' he said curtly.

Faced with his reluctance, Cheska's determination grew.

'I *want* to see it, please. For heaven's sake, it's my only claim to cinematic fame,' she said impatiently, when Lawson hesitated. 'I'm entitled to see it.'

He hesitated for a moment longer, then he sighed. 'Come along in. Can I get you a drink?' he offered, as she went with him indoors.

'No, thanks,' Cheska replied.

As she sat on the sofa, Lawson switched on the television and pressed the 'play' button on the video control.

'Enjoy,' he said, lowering himself into an armchair beside her.

Her gaze fixed on the screen, Cheska watched as a glamorous brunette in a flowing black cape, ultra-short skirt and high heels emerged from the grey stone portals of a turreted Scottish castle. She swung slender black-stockinged legs into a low-slung car, looked up at a window and, glimpsing the shadowy shape of a man, blew him a kiss. Her twenty-one-year-old self turned a key in the ignition. For a moment the camera lingered on her face, on her hands which were clasping the steering-wheel, then the shot changed to show, first, the limousine springing away like a gleaming black panther, then curving sinuously along hairpin mountain roads. A few seconds later, the car executed a risky, but elegant U-turn. A voice-over gave facts on acceleration speeds, braking ability, and made a reference to the dealers—Delaneys—never failing to offer 'that essential bit extra', then came a logo, the Delaney name, and the film was through.

Cheska sat mute. On one level it was impossible not to have enjoyed the commercial, which had been impeccably shot and was beautifully stylish. But. But. It had been odd to watch her younger celluloid image, and even odder to see herself looking so aglow, so sexually sated, so much a woman in love. Her stomach knotted. Was that what her friends had seen when they had heaped praise on the commercial? She knew how she had felt at the time—before her illusions had been torn away—but she had had no inkling that her feelings had been so transparently and embarrassingly *visible*.

She turned to Lawson.

'What was your reason for showing it to Amy?' Cheska enquired, though the coldness which had settled around her heart told her she already knew.

Jabbing a finger on the remote control, he snapped off the TV. 'She doesn't care for Nicholas,' he said, 'and, although she's managed to mask her dislike this far, today, when the action reached the point where she was supposed to be besotted with his character, she froze. As you saw.'

Cheska nodded. She had been there for several of the abortive takes.

'For the past three weeks, Amy's not only been telling me that she wouldn't be able to act as if she loved the guy,' Lawson continued, 'she also insisted she didn't even know how she was expected to act. Which seemed over-the-top and a touch hysterical, but——' He took a mouthful of gin and tonic. 'So last Sunday when I went home to Hampstead, I brought back the tape. I thought it might help as a demonstration.'

The knots in Cheska's stomach tightened. 'A demonstration of what?' Her chin lifted and she forced herself to meet his eyes. 'How besotted I was with you?'

'A demonstration of how besotted the girl in the car was with the man in the window—who, in fact, was the sixty-year-old owner of the castle,' Lawson replied, his brown gaze level on hers. 'And the video did help, because Amy reckons she now understands the kind of mood I'm looking for.'

Cheska's head pounded. And now she understood why first the actor, and then the actress, had spoken as they did. Now she understood that Lawson had been biding his time before he retaliated. Now she understood that she was dealing with a man for whom no holds were barred; though hadn't she known that all along?

'And, as the demonstration proceeded, you just happened to tell Amy and Nicholas how you'd achieved my besotted look—by sleeping with me,' she said, and stopped, her throat tightening.

She felt underpinned, cheated, betrayed. As he had done once before, Lawson Giordano had wounded her and made her bleed—this time by talking about the night they had spent together. How could he have been so callous, so negligent of her feelings, so indifferent? Cheska flinched. Although the facts had insisted otherwise, for five years she had clung on to the tiny stubborn irrational hope that he must have felt *something*, but now that hope had died. His indiscretion proved that Lawson had not cared. Not one bit. And the knowledge crucified.

He frowned. 'I told them——? No.'

'So you dropped heavy hints and they guessed, at which point you felt obliged to reveal all. In glorious Technicolor, no doubt,' Cheska said savagely.

'Whoa,' Lawson protested, 'I seem to be missing a beat or two here. What makes you think that Amy and Nicholas know about our night together?'

She rose to her feet. What did she say? That, having been alerted to their liaison, the actors had put two and two together and come up with five. Come up with the absurd idea that she remained besotted? Cheska frowned. She was not sure why, but she objected to telling him that.

She flung out an arm. 'They've seen the commercial.'

'So?'

'So, while it obviously doesn't bother you, I don't appreciate having the intimate details of my—my personal life bandied around. Call it toffee-nosed, call it old-fashioned, call me a prude, but I prefer such matters to be kept private!'

Lawson stood up. 'You have a very low opinion of me,' he observed.

'I wonder why,' Cheska snapped. 'But did you need to go to the bother of showing Amy the video?' she went on, her tone picking up a needling edge. 'Wouldn't it be more effective if you simply slid her between the sheets with you, too?'

He looked at her. 'You're crazy, you know that?'

'You don't sleep with all your leading ladies?' Cheska gave a brittle laugh. 'My mistake. But you slept with me in order to wrest an appropriate performance out of me, so who knows—it may be worth a spin with Amy.'

Lawson's eyes narrowed into dark slits. 'I slept with you in order to wrest a performance out of you?' he said.

'You didn't think I realised? I did. A slick chick, this one.' There was another brittle laugh. Cheska needed to be flip, she needed to be angry; the only alternative was to burst into tears, and she refused to do that. 'I know that for you anything's permissible in the name of art, but there's no need to punish yourself on my account,' she went on, when his frown deepened, 'because the night was no big deal for me, either. I may have seemed a little...bedazzled the next day, but the feeling didn't last.'

A nerve throbbed in his temple. 'I never thought it had,' Lawson said brusquely. 'After all, at the time you were heavily involved with the Delaney son and heir.' He paused. 'Not that it put any curb on your desire. As I recollect, you——'

'I'd be grateful if you didn't show the video to anyone else,' Cheska cut in, at speed. She did not want to hear his recollections; of how she had slithered, of how eager and shameless and uninhibited she had been. 'All right?'

His eyebrows and his shoulders going up in unison, Lawson gave a very casual, very Latin, shrug. 'Whatever my lady wishes,' he said.

At the words, her control snapped, and her hand rose in the air, but, by his lightning reflex, was deflected before it could make contact.

'Slap me,' Lawson said, his fingers tightening around the slender bones of her wrist, 'and I shall be tempted to retaliate. Quite possibly by tanning your delectable backside. Hard.' Dark brown eyes locked on to hers. 'Understand?'

Cheska seethed in his grasp. She understood a lot of things but, right now, the main one was that she had been beaten. Wrenching free, she crossed to the door in silence and stalked out.

It was so *hot*. Flinging aside the sheet, Cheska rolled on to her back. If only she could fall asleep, but her brain was too active. For the past three hours, thoughts of that insensitive, uncaring, hurtful brute Lawson Giordano had been circling endlessly around in her head. Cheska gazed up into the dark.

All she had ever been to him was a one-night stand—the description set her teeth on edge—whereas he had grabbed her heart. She had cared for the man, and when she had gone to bed with him it had been in the belief that they were at the start of a loving and serious relationship. They might have known each other only a matter of days, and spent those days at odds, yet when he had kissed her she had been struck by an instinctive sense of certainty, a compelling *rightness*, and had thought Lawson had felt it, too. Cheska pummelled her pillow. She had thought wrong.

After spending the night with her and finally shooting a perfect take, Lawson had quit the Scottish Highlands location, flown to London and on to the States. Leaving her besotted, bedazzled, and waiting for a phone call from her new love, who had sworn he would be in touch. But she had never heard from him again. Not a word. It had been a classic case of love 'em and leave 'em, Cheska thought miserably, plucking the gold satin of her nightgown from the heat of her skin. As the lonely, bewildered weeks had dragged by, it had eventually dawned on her that in making love, Lawson had simply been cajoling, making her receptive to his wishes, imprinting on her that soft, sensual look of love which—as she had seen this evening—would be captured so effectively by the camera. Cheska rolled on to her stomach. He had achieved this by being a tender, strong, masterful lover—a wonderful lover—or it had seemed that way. But she had been starry-eyed and, after a fumbling union with a teenage sweetheart,

Lawson had been only the second man she had made love with, so what had she known?

Climbing out of bed, Cheska crossed to the window. Before when he had hurt her she had sobbed herself to sleep for what seemed like a lifetime, but no tears would be shed now. Now she intended to fight back and get even. She gazed out at a rural landscape silvered by a full moon. Her getting even would not just be for his heartless revelation of their affair, but also for all the times, since they had met again, when Lawson had played unnerving games with her equilibrium. Cheska hooked the shoestring strap of her nightgown higher up her shoulder. Having decided to teach him a lesson, all that remained was for her to work out how.

She sighed. Half an hour ago there had been the whirr of her neighbour's shower, but since then nothing so presumably he was asleep. She wished *she* were. Cheska sighed again. Perhaps some fresh air would help?

Quietly letting herself out of the oast, she crossed the patio. As she scrunched her toes in the grass and felt the warmth of the earth beneath her feet, Cheska smiled. She inhaled. Already she felt better. Her nightgown swishing softly around her legs, she started to walk. Whenever she had had 'town' friends to stay they had been wary of the countryside at night, but for her it held no fears. Halfway down the sloping lawn and off to the left was the rectangular swimming pool, with a small changing pavilion at the far end. Wandering over, Cheska sat on the edge and lowered her legs into the shadowy water. In contrast to the warm night air, it felt cool. She kicked her legs and, on impulse, slid her nightgown off over her head. She would have a dip. Cheska swam a few lengths of breaststroke, a couple of energetic backstroke, then tucked herself into a corner at the shallow end. Once again, thoughts of Lawson intruded. When gibing about her lack of loyalty to Justin Delaney, he had described them as being 'heavily involved', but it had not been so. Their relationship had been platonic, superficial, and, indeed, she had terminated it at the time of the commercial. Her face clouded. She felt sure she had explained all that to Lawson.

Cheska flicked a finger in the water. Justin Delaney had been big on image, which was why he had made a beeline for her. Having a pretty model for his girlfriend, one who lived in a manor house to boot, had appealed. She had complemented the Armani suits which the young man wore, the top-of-the-range models of his father's cars which he drove, added gloss to the 'golden-boy' aura which he loved to project. Cheska made a face. As soon as she had realised she was an accessory, she had been ready to split, but Justin had revealed a possessive streak. Accessory or not, she must remain *his*, and without her knowledge he had fixed with his father for her to be the girl in the car commercial. His aim had been to make her grateful and bind her to him, but it had had the opposite effect. Cheska had objected to being skewered into an arrangement about which she knew nothing. She had also resented Justin's coming up to Scotland to act the big I-am and gracious benefactor, and had ended their relationship there and then. Again, she

flicked at the water. The ending had been un-
pleasant for, now revealing a mean streak, the
young man had threatened her with all kinds of
reprisals; though they had never happened.

All of a sudden, Cheska listened. There had been
a rustling among the dark wedge of bushes on the
lower side of the pool, a vigorous rustling. Planting
her feet on the tiles, she stood motionless in the
water. What had it been? Or should the question
be—who? Despite the heat, she shivered. Her heart
began to pound. Abruptly the night *did* hold fears,
and Cheska was awesomely aware of being a woman
alone in the darkness of the countryside. A naked
woman!

Her grey eyes wary, she gazed at the bushes which
were now still. Could someone have been roaming
the moonlit fields, heard her splashes and decided
to investigate? Had she alerted a Peeping Tom? Or
maybe the rapist Lawson had once mentioned? As
headlines of 'young brunette assaulted and
murdered' filled her head, icy fingers of fear ran
down her spine. At the far end of the pool her
nightgown lay in a crumpled golden heap and, with
her head tucked beneath the edge and her hands
sliding along the rail, Cheska made her way swiftly
and noiselessly through the water towards it.

Her intention was to pull on the nightgown and
gallop up to the oast at speed, but as she was
climbing the steps, the bushes moved again. For a
split-second, sheer terror held her rigid, then Cheska
grabbed for the satin. Clutching it to her chest, she
sprinted along the poolside and around the corner
on to the lawn. As she ran, she gazed fearfully back
over her shoulder. Was the Peeping Tom, or the

rapist, or whoever, going to chase her? Would he run faster? Did she have enough of a start on him to——

Cheska screamed. She had been so engrossed in looking behind her, she had not seen what lay ahead and she had run slap-bang into someone. A man, so an instinctive sense of height and size and muscular strength told her. Gooseflesh shivered her skin. She had run slap-bang into the rapist!

'Get away from me!' Cheska shrieked, flailing blindly out with her free arm.

'Careful,' a familiar voice protested, and when she looked up she saw that it was Lawson who was dodging her blows.

Holding her nightgown to her with one hand, Cheska hooked the other around his neck. 'Thank heavens,' she blabbered. 'I thought that whoever it was who'd been watching must have cut round ahead of me somehow and was going to——' She gulped in a breath. 'I've never been more pleased to see anyone in my whole life.'

Lawson looked down at her. 'Odd,' he remarked. 'Earlier I would have sworn you had me tagged as a complete sh—a rat,' he adjusted.

Cheska stepped back. 'Yes, I did,' she admitted.

'But when the *pommes frites* are down and a bit of muscle is required, even rats have their uses?'

She nodded. Though this rat did not have just a bit of muscle, he had a lot. Barefoot and clad in the navy boxer shorts which she had seen in his bedroom, Lawson looked bigger and broader without his clothes. The supreme male animal. Moonlight cast mysterious shadows across the rolling width of his shoulders, and glistened on the dark whorls of body hair; hair which covered his chest and narrowed into a line which went vertically over the flat plane of his belly to vanish into his shorts. Cheska swallowed. Sexual attraction was a strange, uncontrollable urge. Not so long ago she had actively loathed the man, but now just looking at him had squeezed the air from her lungs and was making her feel weak.

'What—what are you doing out here?' she enquired breathlessly.

'I couldn't sleep and as I was looking out of the window, I noticed a movement in the bushes. It seemed as if there could be an intruder.'

'You were worried they might damage the papier mâché flower urns which have been placed around the forecourt?' Cheska enquired, refusing to fall into the trap of thinking that Sir Galahad might have galloped to *her* rescue.

Lawson shook his head. 'I'd heard splashing and realised you were having a swim, and I thought you could be at risk.'

She smiled, feeling comforted and overwhelmingly pleased. She had opened her mouth to thank him when, lower down the lawn, the rustling sound came again. With a gasp of alarm, Cheska launched herself forward, wrapped an arm around his neck and clung on for dear life.

'Oh, no!' she squeaked.

'Some commando,' Lawson remarked drily, then, looking beyond her, he grinned. 'Some risk,' he said, and when she turned her head Cheska saw two foxes and their cub trotting jauntily out of the bushes and away down the lawn.

'I feel a real idiot,' she confessed, and stopped, waiting for what could only be a sardonic reply.

When Lawson said nothing, Cheska turned back to him. His gaze had lowered and when she glanced down, she saw that the nightgown which she had believed was covering her breasts now hung in a straight fall of golden satin between them. She had high firm breasts, their peaks proudly centred in darkly spreading aureoles, and Lawson seemed hypnotised.

'The thought of your breasts, your nipples, has been driving me crazy,' he muttered, and placing his hands on either side of the outer swell of her breasts, he abruptly drew her up and towards him.

Pushing the tip-tilted curves together, he lowered his head, and as she felt the rasp of his tongue across first one tight nipple and then the other, Cheska's senses swam. The earth seemed to vibrate beneath her feet and the air jangled, but then, just as suddenly as he had drawn her near, Lawson held her away.

'Put on your nightgown,' he said harshly.

Bemused, Cheska looked at him. It took her a moment or two to recover, then cogs began to whirr in her brain. When she had kissed him she had thought he had been annoyed because she had taken the initiative, but she had picked up the wrong signal. Now it had become clear that Lawson's annoyance had been because she had aroused him and shaken him, as he was aroused and shaken now.

A smile started to play around her lips. 'But it's wet.' Cheska lowered her arm, and the satin covering fell. 'And I'm wet.'

As if magnetised, his eyes moved over the dampness of her breasts and trailed down her glistening body until they reached the dark triangle of hair at her thighs. Dark curly hair which was threaded through with silvered diamond drops.

Lawson shuddered. 'Sweet mercy,' he breathed, and, as if needing to fight the urge to touch, he balled his fists. His head came up. 'Wet or not,' he said thickly, 'put the damn thing on.'

She did not move. 'Surely a little nakedness doesn't...bother you?' Cheska protested, gazing at him with wide grey eyes. 'You're a man of the world, in the film business for heaven's sake, and, after all, you have seen me naked before.'

'We're out in the open,' he grated, 'and——'

'Here alone, on a balmy summer night.' She trailed a finger down his arm. 'How do you fancy skinny-dipping?'

Snatching his arm away, he snatched the nightgown from her. 'All I fancy is you covering yourself up,' Lawson snarled, and yanked the gold satin over her head. 'Now put it on!'

Cheska slid her arms through the straps and made a great play of wriggling the nightdress down her damp body. 'Whatever my lord wishes,' she said, as she smoothed it over her hips.

Glowering, he jabbed a finger up the lawn. 'Walk! Do you want me to drag you?' he threatened, when she did not immediately move.

Cheska grinned. 'No, I'll come quietly. So the shoot could finish a day or two earlier than planned, weather permitting,' she remarked, her tone leisurely and conversational as they made their way up the grassy slope.

'What?' Lawson said distractedly. 'Yes.'

'And then you'll be off.'

His gaze had been fixed straight ahead, but now
he slung her a sideways glance. 'Not immediately.
I've arranged with Rupert to rent the oast for
another week. I need to spend time deciding the
way I want my career and my life to go.' As they
reached the oasts, he stopped. 'It'd be sensible if
you didn't come out here alone in the dead of
night,' he said.

Her hair hung damp and heavy on her shoulders
and, lifting her arms, Cheska reached up and
smoothed it back into a ponytail.

'You think someone could be tempted to
pounce?' she enquired.

'It's possible.'

Although the action had been unconscious, in
raising her arms, she had lifted her breasts and
Cheska could not help but notice how, for a
fleeting, grudging moment, his eyes had been drawn
to her cleavage.

'Do you think someone being tempted to pounce
is very possible?' she asked, her eyes dancing.
'What do you reckon the chances are—twenty to
one, ten to one, evens?'

'Go to bed,' Lawson grated.

Letting her hair drop, she shone him an impish
smile. 'You're a hard man to say no to.'

There was a mouthful of Italian invective.
'*Francesca,*' he thundered, but the door of her oast
had swung closed behind her.

As she climbed the stairs, Cheska grinned. Now
she knew that she was not the only one who was
susceptible; it worked both ways. And now she
knew *exactly* how to get even!

CHAPTER SIX

As SHE poured herself another cup of coffee, Cheska hummed a little tune. When she had climbed into bed for the second time last night she had fallen asleep within minutes and now, after nine undisturbed hours, she felt bright-eyed, full of zest—and ready to make her plans. A spoonful of sugar was stirred into her cup. What she intended to do was inflame Lawson's desire until it reached the point where he was wild with wanting and almost crying out for release, and then walk coolly away without a backward glance. As he had walked away from her.

She sipped at her coffee. It was inevitable that her own equilibrium must be rocked in the process, yet it had been rocked before and she had survived. But in teaching Lawson a lesson she would also be finally exorcising him and healing the scar, and then she would be able to continue with the rest of her life unperturbed.

She did not want to alert her victim to her manipulation and scare him off, Cheska reflected, so her inflammatory tactics must be more subtle than the *outré* nightgown-shedding of last night. And, as she had no wish to be perceived as pursuing Lawson by others, they would be restricted to when the two of them were alone. She rested an elbow on the kitchen table. Over the evenings of the next three weeks she would keep his sexual awareness of her simmering and, once the film was complete and the crew had departed, turn up the heat. High. Cheska's lips curved. She had never acted the siren before—on the contrary, she seemed to have spent much of her life fighting men off— but she could imagine no greater satisfaction than to reduce Lawson Giordano to an imploring, quivering, frustrated wreck!

The sudden shrill of the bell sliced into her thoughts. Could this be her intended victim now? Cheska wondered, as she went through to open the door. It was. In an open-necked brown shirt and sand-coloured corduroys, Lawson looked composed and masterful, clearly not a man with an identity crisis. Her pulse-rate quickened. As it always did, his strong physical presence hit her with a thud, somewhere in the solar plexus.

'Sleep well?' Cheska asked brightly, her nerves starting to twang as she thought of her plans to inflame him.

'Not very.'

She angled him a look. 'It was a hot night; perhaps you needed a cold shower?'

'What I need,' Lawson rasped, looking unamused, 'is a year-old baby.'

'Excuse me?'

'I can't understand how I could have overlooked it,' he said, starting to gesture with his hands, 'but I've been doing the preparation for the scene we're to shoot on Monday and I've suddenly realised that we need——'

'A baby boy with blond hair and blue eyes, who's supposed to be Nicholas's character's illegitimate son, and who'll be glimpsed for one brief but crucial moment. It's all arranged,' Cheska informed him.

'It is?' Lawson said, in surprise.

She nodded. 'I was going to tell you. When I read the script I noticed there was to be a shot of a baby,' she explained, 'so I checked with Casting and, when they didn't seem to know anything about it, fixed up with a friend in Soper's Corner to use her son. It seemed silly to pay through the nose for a baby to be brought specially down from London.'

'Very.'

'And Jill doesn't want any fee, she says the chance to see Nicholas Preston in the flesh will be payment enough.' Cheska pulled a face. 'Though I thought we ought to send her some flowers or maybe a gift token.'

'Whichever,' Lawson agreed, and grinned. 'Thanks for picking up on it.'

'That's why I'm being paid my inflated salary,' she told him pertly. 'Would you like to take a look at the baby?' she carried on. 'Jill and her husband run the newsagents' shop and I was going to drive into the village in a few minutes to get a paper.'

'I'm sure the baby'll be fine,' he said, 'but I'll come with you and get a couple of papers myself. Jill's a small, plump, fair girl?' She nodded. 'I've spoken to her when I've been in the shop and——' Lawson adopted a pained expression '—been treated to endless snippets of local gossip.'

'Jill does tend to chatter,' Cheska agreed ruefully.

'I never realised he was Lawson Giordano,' Jill whispered, as she lifted her small son out of his playpen which was parked at the back of the shop.

'I knew he had far more oomph than our usual run of customer, but I had no idea I was serving a world-famous film director.'

'He's not *that* famous,' Cheska protested, for her friend was almost jigging up and down in her excitement.

'He will be,' Jill asserted, and gazed down through the gondolas of cards and confectionery to where Lawson was paying her husband for the newspapers. 'He's dishy.'

'As dishy as Nicholas Preston?' she enquired drily.

'Almost, but not quite,' said the devoted fan. Wetting her fingers, she flicked her son's fair hair up into a curl. 'This is your big chance,' she informed him, 'so smile.'

When he was carried over to be displayed, the baby did smile. He also lurched forward, grabbed hold of Lawson's shirt collar in a chubby fist and held on tight.

'You're going to be a real star,' Lawson said, lifting him into his arms.

'You think so?' Jill asked, as the baby attempted to stuff the point of his collar into his mouth.

'He'll steal the scene,' he replied.

The young mother beamed with pleasure and pride.

Watching how Lawson had so spontaneously taken the child and was tickling his tummy, Cheska felt a catch form in her throat. She knew that Italians were reputed to be fond of children, but she had never seen that fondness in action before, and she found the cameo of the tall man playing so easily with the unknown baby strangely affecting.

Could it be because it prompted her to imagine Lawson as a father? Cheska wondered. As the father of *her* child? The pill she had religiously taken—and took now—meant there had been no risk of her becoming pregnant five years ago, yet she found the prospect interesting, disturbing, provocative...

'Are you still in the market for secondhand baby clothes?' Jill enquired.

Cheska snapped her thoughts back to attention. She must be getting broody.

'Please,' she said. 'Although I'm not with the charity any longer, I can still arrange for items to be sent out.'

Lawson raised surprised brows. 'You were working for a charity in Thailand?' he enquired.

'She was, and it was a no-frills operation so her living conditions were basic. Not quite a tin hut in the jungle, but almost,' Jill said, jumping in first. 'When Cheska told us she'd applied for the job, we were astonished, too. Couldn't imagine her doing anything so lowly.'

Cheska bridled. 'Why not?' she demanded.

Her friend grinned. 'You did used to be a bit high-falutin.'

'No, I didn't,' she started to protest, but out of the mists of time swam a recollection of a younger Francesca. While today she wore a simple white vest, khaki shorts and trainers, with a flick of mascara as her only cosmetic, a few years ago she would not have been seen dead that way. Then, she used to come into the village with her face immaculately made-up, clad in some expensive high-fashion outfit, and would—she squirmed at the memory—parade. And, while she had been friends with other village children like Jill, she had secretly considered herself to be superior. Far superior, if she was honest. 'Yes, I did,' she conceded guiltily.

'It was understandable,' Jill said, with a smile, and turned to Lawson. 'Rupert had always let her do whatever she wanted to do, and treated her like a princess,' she explained, 'so you can't blame Cheska if she started to act that way. He should have been stricter and cut her down to size, but I think he was compensating for what had happened with his sister and, of course, for——'

'His sister?' Lawson cut in sharply.

'Rupert had a sister, Sylvie, who caused a family scandal,' Jill said. 'She——'

'You're needed,' Cheska told her.

The shop had been quiet, but a couple of customers had just walked in and Jill's husband was beckoning that he required her help. Thank goodness, Cheska thought wryly. Her friend had been bursting to regale Lawson, but they were only here to buy papers and having her character dissected and analysed had already been enough, without spending another half-hour listening to tales of the skeletons which lurked in the Finch's family's cupboard.

With a sigh of resignation, the young mother took back her son and returned him to his playpen. 'Do you two have anything planned for today?' she enquired, glancing out at the warm yellow sunshine which bathed the village street. 'Give me half a chance and I'd be off for a picnic.'

'Sounds like a good idea,' Lawson said, and looked at Cheska. 'What do you think?'

She thought that the bits of washing and cleaning which she had intended to do could wait, and that a picnic would give her an opportunity to set his sexual awareness gently simmering.

'I'd like that,' Cheska agreed, with a smile. 'We can buy cheese and fruit and whatever else we need, while we're here in the village.'

'What happened about Chen?' Jill asked abruptly, when they had said their goodbyes and were turning to leave. 'He was a widower with six children who was desperate to run his own taxi. Cheska wrote me a worried letter about him,' she told Lawson. 'Did the charity manage to find enough money for him to put a down-payment on a car?'

Cheska shook her head. 'I'm afraid not.'

'So you financed him?' her friend declared. 'Down to your last bean.'

'I had to,' she protested.

'You're a big softie,' Jill said, hugging her, and finally went off to help her husband.

Tipping back his head Lawson took a swig of ice-cold beer, then he wiped his mouth with the back of his hand and returned the can to the cool box. 'Bliss,' he proclaimed, as he lay back in the long grass.

Sitting cross-legged beside him, Cheska lifted up her arms and stretched. 'Isn't it?' she agreed.

Their picnic lunch had been eaten and the mood was lazy. Long shafts of sunlight pierced the overhead canopy of trees to dapple the greenery around them, while, below, brightly coloured dragonflies hung over the surface of the pool. The countryside dozed, silent and still, in the heat of the afternoon. Cheska gave a happy sigh. Although, in her travels, she had visited tropical white-sand beaches, breathtaking hill country, exquisite palm-fringed lakes, she had never found any place she would rather be than at Hatchford Manor. It had been a much needed constant in her life when she was growing up, and even now represented stability. She gazed up through the trees. Just looking at the house made her feel comfortable inside.

All of a sudden, Lawson pushed himself up on one elbow. 'Does your helping the man, Chen, mean that you are working in order to eat?' he enquired.

'Yes,' Cheska said simply.

'Did you break some rule by giving him your own money? Was that the reason why you left?'

'No, I left because I was under pressure from my boss.' She stared down at the dark green water. 'He told me he wanted to marry me, but he was already married, with three young children.'

Lawson frowned. 'This is why you got so steamed up when I accused you of messing around with Nicholas three weeks back?'

She nodded. 'What happened in Thailand distressed me and my feelings were raw. Are still raw.'

'Would it help if you talked about it?' he suggested.

Breaking off a blade of grass, Cheska chewed pensively at the sweet tip. She had given Rupert, and anyone else who had asked, a fudged story about the charity no longer being able to afford a secretary. But now, although she had not envisaged revealing the truth, let alone using Lawson as a confidant, the chance to talk suddenly seemed attractive.

'I think it could,' she agreed, then hesitated, not knowing where to begin.

'What was your boss called?' Lawson prompted.

'Frank.'

'How old was he?'

'Forty-five. When I first went to Thailand, I worked for him and another man, and for the first two years Frank's attitude towards me was simply that of a colleague,' Cheska said, starting to ease herself into her dialogue. 'And vice versa. I liked him and we operated fine on the work level, but it never occurred to me to think of him in romantic terms. After all, he was married, and middle-aged, and overweight.' She tossed the blade of grass aside. 'However, two years ago the other man retired and wasn't replaced, which left Frank and me far more on our own. Gradually I began to notice how he was spending a lot of his time just gazing at me. Then he started to say how lovely I was and soon it reached the stage where every day he'd make some personal remark, pay some lavish compliment.'

'Which must have made you feel uncomfortable,' Lawson observed.

Cheska nodded. 'And under pressure. His wife had stayed in England with the children,' she continued, 'though once a year she'd come out to Thailand, and she was so nice. And when she was there, Frank seemed devoted to her.' Stretching out her legs, Cheska turned over on to her stomach and lay beside him. 'Anyhow, about six months ago,

Frank suddenly declared that he was in love with me and he knew I cared for him. I was shocked. Stunned. I told him he was mistaken and that his feelings were not reciprocated; I also reminded him that he was married, and, as far as I was concerned, that was the end of the story. For a while it seemed that way——'

'He stopped gazing?' Lawson interrupted.

'No, but he never said anything else and so I began to feel easier. Then one evening about a month ago when we were in Bangkok to meet some international aid people, Frank barged his way into my hotel room.' Cheska's expression tightened. 'He told me he understood how, because he was married, I'd been unwilling to admit that I cared, but there was no need to hold back any longer because he was going to ask his wife for a divorce.'

'Oh, hell,' Lawson muttered.

'Frank seemed to think that also meant I'd be happy to hop into bed and he started pawing me.' Cheska shuddered at the memory. 'I insisted that I didn't love him and said I had no intention of sleeping with him, and because we were in a hotel and I'd begun to state my objections rather forcibly——'

'I can imagine,' Lawson said drily.

'—he went away. But I couldn't have him divorcing his wife on my account, and I couldn't risk him barging in on me again—and I felt *trapped*!' she wailed. 'So the next morning I decided the only solution was to leave.'

'It was the right decision,' he said.

'I agree,' Cheska said, and smiled. Talking to Lawson had been therapeutic and she felt . . . eased.

'But it means that now not only am I without a permanent job, but I'm picky.'

'Picky?'

'From now on, I'll only work for a confirmed bachelor or a woman—or a robot,' she added.

Lawson laughed. 'Whichever it is, I'd be happy to provide a glowing reference.'

'So you agree that I can do everything Janet can do?' Cheska enquired eagerly.

'That's a tough one; you'll have to give me a minute,' he said, and retrieving his can, he proceeded to take a long and agonisingly slow swig of beer.

'Tell me!' she demanded, itching to know.

Lawson returned the can to the cool box. 'You said you were the best, and you are.'

'Honest?'

'Cross my heart and hope to die.'

Cheska knew it was foolish, yet she felt like turning cartwheels and bursting into song. For a minute or two, she wallowed in his praise, then her expression became pensive.

'You know Jill reckoned I was high falutin?' she said. 'I think that, subconsciously, I realised I was becoming a bit uppity, and that's one of the reasons why I applied for the charity job. It took me away from Rupert's spoiling and demanded discipline, plus it promised to be...down-to-earth and grounding.'

'You seem grounded now,' Lawson told her. 'But there were times during the making of the commercial when you were very uppity.'

'Was that the impression I gave?' Cheska asked uncertainly.

Reaching out a long arm, he wrapped it around her waist and drew her close, fitting her against him. 'Fraid so,' he said.

As she felt the heat of his body coming through his clothes and smelled the clean male scent of him, Cheska suddenly realised that, this far, she had not made a single stab at raising his sexual consciousness. It was a situation which needed to be rectified.

Placing her hand on his chest, she slipped a finger between the buttons on his shirt. 'So that's why you call me ''my lady''?' she enquired, and, with what was intended to seem like abstracted idleness, she started to caress his skin.

'It is. Jill talked about Rupert compensating for what happened with his sister,' Lawson went on, his tone becoming grave. 'What did she mean?'

'Rupert felt that he didn't support Sylvie enough at her time of need and so, when it came to me, he went overboard.'

He frowned. 'What was Sylvie's time of need?' he questioned.

Removing her finger, Cheska shifted away. She did not want the mood to be serious, she thought impatiently; she needed it to be light, bantering, flirtatious. She cast him a sideways look. Lawson could have no real interest in Rupert's sister, so did his sobriety mean he had realised what she had in mind and was foiling her? If so, her next approach would need to be even more casual, more understated.

'I don't know the details, because it happened long before my time and Rupert prefers not to talk about it, but Sylvie fell in love with someone whom her mother felt was beneath her. Apparently Beatrice Finch was an avid social climber with very grand ideas,' Cheska explained, rattling out the words, 'and when Sylvie said she wanted to marry the man, she forbade it.'

Lawson pushed himself up into a sitting position. 'But Desmond Finch didn't?' he queried.

'I don't think he minded who Sylvie married so long as she was happy, but Beatrice seems to have ruled the roost, so——' Cheska's shoulders rose and fell. 'However, not much later, Sylvie announced that she was pregnant, at which point her mother threw her out of the house.'

'And Desmond let her? You said he was gentle, but to me the man sounds to have been an ineffectual, inadequate, cowardly swine!'

Cheska looked at him in surprise. Lawson's expression was tense and condemnation burned in his eyes. She knew he possessed his share of strong Latin emotions, but surely this was going over the top?

'I understand Desmond was away on a business trip at the time,' she explained, 'so he didn't know what Beatrice had done. However, the moment he realised he went round to the house where Sylvie's boyfriend had been living to ask her to come home, but they'd gone. Desmond attempted to find out where, but no one knew—or if they did, they weren't telling. After a couple of weeks or so, Rupert received a letter from his sister to say she was married, though she gave no address, and several months later her husband wrote informing him that she'd died just a few hours after the birth of their child. That was the last anyone ever heard.'

'Why did Rupert feel he'd been unsupportive?' Lawson demanded.

'Because he was present when his mother threw Sylvie out and he didn't prevent it. I gather that although Beatrice had always dominated him, he argued and insisted that what she was doing was wrong, though she refused to listen. But afterwards Rupert felt he hadn't argued hard enough and that he'd let his sister down. He was only eighteen or nineteen at the time, but it's plagued him ever since.'

'Beatrice Finch must have had a heart of stone,' Lawson said bitterly.

'She sounds as if she was a monster,' Cheska agreed. 'When Desmond made efforts to trace Sylvie's husband and the baby——'

'He tried?' he demanded.

'Yes, though without success. Yet apparently Beatrice had said that even if the baby was delivered to her door she wouldn't see it.'

'How could anyone do that?' Lawson demanded, in an anguished voice.

'Don't get so uptight,' she protested.

'But it was her own daughter's child, her grandchild!'

Cheska frowned. His expression was strained and his eyes were hard, their irises dark with deep-felt emotion. Maybe it was because Lawson was usually so composed and in command, but his distress wrapped itself around her heart.

'All this happened a long time ago,' she said soothingly.

'You don't understand,' he rasped, then stopped.

'I don't understand what?' Cheska asked, for she had had the impression he had been about to say something important, though she could not be sure.

Lawson shook his head. 'This isn't a day for agonising over the injustices of the world,' he said, and started unfastening his shirt.

The buttons undone, he put the shirt aside and lay down again on his back. As if drawn by a magnet, Cheska's eyes went to his bare chest—to the golden muscles, to the flat brown pebbles of his nipples, to the matt of dark hair.

Lawson smiled. 'I've made it easier for you,' he said.

Cheska pinkened, aware she had been staring. 'Made what easier?' she enquired, a touch breathlessly.

'Your seduction. Instead of sliding just one finger into my shirt, you can stroke your hands all over me.'

Cheska's pink cheeks became scarlet. He had realised what she had been attempting to do, but instead of foiling he was now actively encouraging!

'I—don't want to seduce you,' she faltered.

Lifting a hand, Lawson twisted a curl of her hair around his finger. 'Of course you do,' he said, with a smile. 'Except that it would only be seduction if I weren't as willing as you are, which doesn't happen to be the case.'

She regarded him with wary eyes. What was he saying? Could this be some kind of a trick, a devious way of underpinning her yet again?

'No?' Cheska said suspiciously.

'No. Oh, I've tried to fight it, but what's the use? Your memory's been haunting me for the past five years.'

She looked at him in wonderment. 'It has?'

'I've never forgotten you. Never,' Lawson vowed, toying with her hair.

'But——'

'Why do you think I kissed you when I pulled you out of the pond here?' he demanded. 'It was because I couldn't stop myself. Because I needed to discover whether I'd been fooling myself all this time or whether the touch of you, the taste of you, still had the power to drive me to distraction. It did. It does.' Sliding his hand around the back of her head, he drew her closer. 'Cheska, I want to make love to you,' he murmured. 'I *need* to.'

Cheska listened to the sound of her heart beating. Keep calm, keep cool, she commanded herself. Everything was going far faster than anticipated or wanted, and not at all as she had planned, yet hadn't she arrived at the desired effect? Yes. Which meant that she must now deliver a put-down, rise to her feet and walk——

'Don't look at me with those big eyes,' Lawson chided, when she sat mute. 'I also have a healthy libido, though it's a darn sight more selective than Nicholas's.'

'You don't advance on everything which isn't mineral?' Cheska asked, hastily sidetracking, for she had realised that if she put him down too harshly it would sour their next three weeks in working harness and she was reluctant for that to happen. A jokey inoffensive put-down was needed, but, hard as she tried to think, one refused to spring to mind.

He shook his head. 'In this day and age that could be suicidal. Seven years ago I was involved in a live-in relationship,' he went on, 'but since then I've——'

'Why did the relationship break up?' Cheska enquired, furiously wondering what she could say.

'With hindsight, I think it was because the girl was too...docile,' Lawson said, and rubbed a tapered finger broodingly across his lower lip. 'I like a woman with her own thoughts, her own identity and, ultimately I suppose, with the ability to make me jealous.'

When he was thoughtful, Lawson had a habit of touching his mouth, and Cheska found her eyes drawn to the movement of his golden-skinned finger. He was stroking it back and forth across the full lip which, she remembered in a vivid, almost physical recollection, she had once caught between her teeth. And when she had released him, he had kissed her hard and long and bruisingly, in glorious punishment. Cheska looked away. To her dismay, she could feel her breasts swelling and tightening at the memory and, too late, wished that she had worn a bra.

'The girl didn't do that?' she asked.

'No,' Lawson replied. 'Since then, although I haven't lived like a monk, neither have I had numerous affairs.'

'So how many girlfriends have you had?'

'Are you intending to try and keep me talking until the sun goes down?' he enquired, looking at

her with an intensity which drove the colour into
her cheeks.

'I don't know what you mean,' Cheska said
evasively.

His gaze remained levelled on her. 'You know
exactly what I mean,' Lawson said, and drawing
her against him, his mouth covered hers.

As she tasted the faint trace of beer on his breath
and felt the moist caress of his tongue, the beat of
Cheska's heart broke into an erratic rhythm. She
kissed him back—what else could she do?—but
when the kiss ended, and she attempted to collect
her thoughts, the lowering of his head distracted
her. Lawson had taken hold of the edge of her vest
and was sliding it up her body, kissing the honeyed
skin as it was revealed. Cheska's eyelids fluttered
closed. The feel of his mouth was making a heat
radiate through her, a heat which had nothing to
do with the sunshine and high temperature, and
everything to do with desire. And with the heat
came an ache, a gnawing reminder of how long it
was since she had last experienced that ultimate
rapture and how ripe she was for love.

Cheska opened her eyes. She swallowed down a
breath. 'Lawson,' she began unsteadily.

The erotic onslaught on her flesh ceased and he
raised his head. 'You'd rather we went indoors?'
he asked.

She gazed at him. This was the time to say she
would rather everything *stopped*. Period. This was
the time to leap to her feet, make that quip and
depart.

'No, but what I——'

Her speech dried and Cheska did not move. She could not move, for he had begun kissing her again. Kissing her stomach, her ribcage and now—the white cotton was peeled upwards—her breasts. As she felt his teeth clamp lightly on to her nipple, Cheska shuddered and arched her back, needing to bite her lips so that she did not call out. Lawson suckled at the sensitive rose-brown peak and then, with an incoherent murmur, he drew the vest over her head. His eyes dark and languorous with longing, he gazed down at her.

'For the past three weeks I've been having the greatest difficulty keeping my hands off of you,' he said thickly.

'You—you have?' Cheska asked hesitantly.

'It's been hell,' Lawson told her.

All ideas of leaving had gone. Now her only awareness was of the grass beneath the length of her spine and the man whose hands were covering the firm globes of her breasts. Lawson curled his fingers around her nipples and rolled them until Cheska gasped and strained closer, wanting more of his touch, and more. Telling her how much he wanted her, how much he needed her, Lawson kissed and caressed her breasts, until, wanting more, too, he pulled back. Together they removed her shorts, and the white lace briefs she wore beneath—though his urgency was such that he made no comment on them—then he stripped off the remainder of his clothes.

As Lawson lay down with her again and she felt the pulsing shaft of his arousal against her, Cheska's insides turned to liquid. His dark head lowered and he moved gradually down her body, kissing her stomach, her hips and the silk-smooth flesh of her thighs. He pressed his mouth to the thatch of dark curls and, as he separated her and touched her with his tongue, she trembled and cried out his name.

The heat had become a raging flood and when Lawson moved up her body again to kiss her mouth, his tongue driving deep, Cheska sucked on it. Eager to return the pleasure he had given her, she pulled back to kiss his throat, his chest, his nipples, staying on them until he groaned a protest and rolled her beneath him. With one thrust he entered her and, as she felt the power of him inside her, Cheska's hips began to move. Sweat sleeked their bodies, a rhythm built—a compelling rhythm, measured at first, but Lawson's thrusts became higher, harder, faster.

'I can't ... we must ... *Cheska*,' he said, in a low guttural voice.

Her fingernails scoring his back, she clung to him. He had brought her to the edge, that tantalising, punishing, unstoppable edge, and as his hips jerked and she felt a rush of molten heat within her, Cheska toppled down, down, down, caught in a swirling, pulsing maelstrom of emotion which finally delivered her, sobbing and panting, on the shores of fulfilment.

'How long is it since you last made love?' Lawson enquired, as they lay together afterwards. 'Sweetheart, I know it must be a long time,' he said, when she hesitated, 'because you were so aroused, so ... ready.'

'It's five years,' Cheska told him.

He pulled away to look at her. 'You don't mean——?'

'Yes, the last time was with you.'

'Oh, Cheska,' Lawson muttered, as though she had given him a precious gift, and he held her close again.

When their hearts had quietened and their bodies had dried, they made love again, and by the time they returned to the oasts the shadows had begun to lengthen.

'Unbolt the door on your landing,' Lawson instructed, as he sat the cool box down in the kitchen of Cheska's house. 'And I'll do the same with mine.'

'Unbolt it?' she questioned.

Wrapping an arm around her waist, he brushed his lips across her brow. 'You can't think that I'm willing to spend my nights alone, now? I'm not. From now on we sleep together, in either your bed or mine. Which is it to be?'

'Um . . . yours.'

Lawson kissed her brow again. 'Fine. I'd prefer not to have everyone gossiping about us on the set,' he went on, 'so let's stick to our working relationship in public and keep the loving private.'

'Whatever you wish,' Cheska said helplessly.

CHAPTER SEVEN

OBLIVIOUS to the winding country lane and the verdant green of the hedgerows, Cheska gazed out through the windscreen. Every night for the past week Lawson had taken her into his bed and made love to her, and every morning she had vowed that it would be for the last time. The same vow had been made this morning, yet a traitorous ache deep inside her warned that all he would need to do this evening was to kiss her and she would go willingly and helplessly to his bed again. A pulse hammered at the base of her throat. How was it possible to long for and yet dread the same thing?

Cheska slid a look at the man who held the wheel beside her; held it with the strong capable fingers which carried her nightly into that wild paradise. Why had she ever dreamed up the skewed notion of seducing him? she wondered, as she had wondered a hundred times before. At the time the concept had seemed plausible, but now it could be recognised as reckless and imprudent, if not foolishness on the grandest of scales. With a singular lack of vision she had ignored a crucial fact—that the sexual fire which had flamed white-hot between them in the past could, would, had always been destined to flame white-hot again. Keeping the awareness 'simmering' had never been an option, not a realistic one.

146

At first, she had been unable to understand what seemed her pathological inability to call an end to their nights together, Cheska brooded. Lawson was a considerable lover, just as tender and powerful as she remembered, but was the sexual bliss which he gave her the only reason why she could not resist? A pain, as sharp as a stiletto, pierced her breast. If only it were that simple. But now she recognised that she had made the same mistake she had made in the past, the mistake she had vowed she would not repeat—she had gone to bed with him *and*, even worse, she had fallen in love with him. Or was it more a case of her never having fallen out of love? Cheska wondered disconsolately. Could she be the victim of a faithful heart? It seemed possible. But loving Lawson was what put her at his mercy and was why, night after night, she knew the ecstasy... and the agony.

Cheska tweaked fretfully at the full sleeve of the copper-coloured blouson top she wore with a slim white skirt. Her lover never spoke of love. He spoke in terms of need and desire and *now*, never of the future. Of course, it was early days and maybe... Wise up, she ordered herself in exasperation. There is no future, not with Lawson. In three weeks' time he'll walk away without a backward glance, as he did before. Cheska gave an ironic smile. Five years ago she had bewailed his going, but now she would be grateful. Grateful to be released from her addiction. She frowned. Her need for him—a man who did not return her love—troubled her constantly. It wrecked her image of herself as a self-sufficient, independently minded woman. It wrecked her peace of mind.

In all of this, there was only one consolation, Cheska reflected—that, as she could not resist him, so Lawson was equally unable to resist her. She had wanted to control him and now, because he desired her in the lusting, besotted, longing-to-possess-her sense, on a physical level she did. Her insides hollowed. It was a dark victory.

'It's kind of Miriam to invite us over to Sunday lunch,' Lawson observed, as he swung the silver Mercedes smoothly around a corner.

'Very,' Cheska replied briefly.

He cast her a look. 'You're not happy about her relationship with Rupert?' he enquired.

'I don't mind it,' she replied, thinking that it was *their* relationship she felt unhappy about. 'Miriam may be sickeningly cheerful——'

'It's a wonder to me how the woman's escaped strangulation all these years,' Lawson remarked drily.

'—but she is good-hearted. She's obviously fond of Rupert and he seems fond of her, so if they do pair up they have my blessing.' Cheska hesitated. 'Let's keep things . . . casual at Miriam's,' she said.

Lawson frowned out at the road ahead. 'You want us to act as if we're just friends?' he enquired.

'Please.'

He moved his shoulders. 'Your choice.'

His act would deceive their hostess and Rupert as completely as it had deceived the film's cast and crew, Cheska mused, as they neared their destination. Lawson seemed to possess an internal switch which he flicked and became her employer, only her employer. A sigh escaped. Although she, too, wanted their involvement to remain a secret, contrarily Cheska had found herself violently wishing for just one lingering smile, one tangling of eyes, one fleeting touch. *Something* from him. There had been nothing—and so she had responded by stalwartly maintaining her own impersonal businesslike stance.

Miriam Shepherd lived in a cottage which, although it was of the clichéd chocolate-box variety, possessed great charm. It had a thatched roof, pristine white walls and mullioned windows. A carefully trained purple clematis grew around the door and the garden was planted with neat clumps of pink and white begonias, marigolds and tall purple-blue hollyhocks. On one corner of the manicured lawn stood a thatched wishing well.

As Lawson drew his Mercedes to a halt in the lane outside, the front door of the cottage opened and Miriam teetered out along the crazy-paving path. Her champagne-blonde head was suavely coiffed, and she wore a bright tangerine-on-white flowered dress and her regulation wide smile. Rupert, who was also smiling, ambled after her, a quieter figure in a white shirt and grey flannels. As she greeted him, Cheska decided that it was a long time since she had seen her stepbrother looking so relaxed. She wished she felt the same.

With much chat and joviality, their hostess welcomed them into her beautifully furnished living-room, through a spotless state-of-the-art kitchen, and out to sit on cushioned chairs on the flower-garlanded rear lawn. Glasses of sherry were served. There was some small talk about the continuing good weather and the film, then Rupert cleared his throat.

'I've reached a decision on Hatchford Manor,' he announced. 'I'm going to sell.'

Askance, Cheska gazed at him. 'Oh, no!' she protested. Because Rupert had said nothing, she had convinced herself that he must be seriously investigating at least one of the money-making schemes which she had suggested, and so the news came as a bitter disappointment.

Her stepbrother stretched across to comfortably pat her hand. ''But not the oasts. They're to be yours.'

'Mine?' Cheska said, in confusion.

'You can live in one and make a little money by renting out the other,' Miriam informed her.

'That way you'll still be on home ground,' Rupert said, 'while I——' he beamed at Miriam' '—live here with my bride.'

'You're getting married?' she asked.

'In two months' time,' Rupert revealed.

'At St Swithin's, with a full choir and a reception for sixty at the Mayfly,' Miriam twittered.

'Congratulations,' Lawson said.

'Yes, that's great news,' Cheska agreed, with a smile.

'Will you bring out the champagne, Rupie dear?' Miriam requested, and he hastened to do her bidding.

Toasts were drunk, and for a while the conversation centred on the wedding. Miriam seemed to already have it organised down to the last detail, which prompted Cheska to wonder—perhaps a touch uncharitably—if her plans had been made two years ago and she had been updating them ever since.

'I've arranged for an estate agent who specialises in large country houses to value Hatchford Manor as soon as the film is finished,' Rupert revealed, as they took their places around the table for lunch. 'Once that's done, a glossy brochure will be produced and the property will be put up for sale.'

'You don't need to go to the expense of a brochure,' Lawson said. 'I'll buy the house.'

Cheska's head swung round and she stared at him. He wanted to buy Hatchford Manor? Her mind seemed to implode. If she owned the oasts and Lawson became the manor house's new laird, then their lives could intermingle and they would be bound to meet. Meet this year, next year, the year after... But she had to escape him, she thought feverishly. She could not spend forever in thrall.

'You'll buy the manor for the price at which it's valued?' Miriam demanded, showing her usual keen attention to money.

Lawson nodded. 'I will.'

'That'd be wonderful,' Rupert said, and gave a great smile of relief.

As grapefruit segments and, later, fresh salmon with new potatoes and garden peas were served, Cheska reeled from the shock of being faced with what could only be a disastrous situation. But by the time the dessert of home-grown raspberries and cream had been eaten, she had thought of a way to extricate herself. And when a chance arose for her to put her thoughts into action, she took it.

'I'm sorry, but I can't accept the oasts,' Cheska said, as she and Rupert sat together in the living-room, drinking coffee.

In response to Lawson's compliments on the dessert, Miriam had bustled him outside to display the splendour of her raspberry canes, and so they were alone.

'Of course you can,' Rupert replied.

Cheska shook her head. 'I appreciate your generosity, appreciate it very much, but I'm not a Finch and, in so many ways, you've given me more than enough already.'

'And I'm giving you the oasts,' he said gently.

'I have no right to them,' she protested.

'You have every right. My father would have wanted it,' he declared. 'Both in appreciation of the love which your mother gave to him and——' he smiled at her '—because he was so fond of you himself.'

Cheska sighed. 'Rupert——'

'I've made up my mind,' he told her. 'The oasts are to be your inheritance.'

Frowning, she sipped at her coffee. He was not going to allow her to refuse, so what did she do? How could she evade Lawson?

'I suppose I could sell them,' Cheska muttered, thinking out loud.

'Sell the oasts?' Rupert protested.

Guilt flooded through her. He had sounded hurt, but she could not hurt him. She could not fling his gift away. She loved him too much.

'I wouldn't. I won't,' Cheska said assuringly, and squeezed his arm. 'I promise.'

The realisation that all she had left was to either dissuade Rupert from selling Hatchford Manor or dissuade Lawson from buying it preoccupied Cheska for the remainder of the visit. She went through the motions of conversation, but all the time she was thinking, thinking. And getting nowhere.

'I have some ironing to do,' she said, when Lawson had parked the Mercedes in the yard and they were making their way round to the oasts.

'And I need to check through the scene which we'll be shooting tomorrow. After such a big lunch I intend to skip dinner,' he went on.

'Me, too,' Cheska inserted.

'So suppose I bring round a bottle of wine in, say, an hour?'

She summoned up a smile. 'Fine.'

In the kitchen, Cheska set up the ironing board and plugged in the iron. Even if she didn't live at the oasts permanently, her ownership must require her to visit from time to time, she mused, and then all it would need was for Lawson to crook his little finger and... The iron was slammed fiercely down and a shirt-front pressed. Was it carved on tablets of stone that when he beckoned she had to respond? No. No. *No*. Cheska ironed like someone possessed. Her attitude was pathetic, a disgrace. She had a will of her own, didn't she? Yes, and all it needed to end their affair, now and for always, was for her to bolt her side of the communal doors upstairs. Simple. Granted, her action would put a strain on the final fortnight of filming, but she could live with that. What she could not live with— what scared her half to death—was the prospect of her addiction to Lawson turning into a long running year-after-year saga.

Everything ironed, Cheska set the iron aside to cool. Her shirts and blouses were ready to be hung in the wardrobe and, at the same time, she would shoot the bolts. She was lifting the pile of clothes when the door bell rang. Her pulse quickened. Although only forty minutes had gone by, this would be Lawson. The upstairs communal door might provide free access and yet, night-times apart, he respected her privacy and always asked to be invited in. She did likewise. Cheska put down the clothes. When she locked her side of the door he would protest—vigorously—so she might as well bite the bullet and advise him of her intention now. She was not sure how she would explain, but she had to make it understood that, from here on, she would be spending her nights alone.

'You're early,' Cheska remarked, when she opened the door.

Lawson gave a crooked grin. 'Couldn't keep away a moment longer.'

Sensing that he was about to reach for her, she swiftly turned and walked ahead of him into the kitchen.

'You need a corkscrew,' she said.

'Sorry?'

'A corkscrew, to open that,' Cheska said, indicating the bottle of white wine which he carried. 'I'll get one.'

With rentals in mind, Miriam had equipped the oasts with just about everything which the discerning tenant could possibly need, from a garlic press to napkin rings to a small dishwasher, and Cheska could remember seeing a corkscrew— somewhere. She opened drawers, searched on shelves, knelt to investigate the lower cupboards of the pine dresser which stood against one wall.

'Success!' she said eventually, but when she offered the corkscrew to Lawson he ignored it.

'I do like the way your skirt stretches over your backside when you bend,' he murmured, curling two arms around her. 'I do like your backside.' Lifting a hand, he caressed her face with his fingers, awakening her nerves. 'I do like you.'

Cheska gazed up at him. Help! squeaked a little voice in her head. Help! All it needed was one touch and a fierce need, a longing, a giddy exhilaration, swept through her. Cool it, instructed another, snappier voice; Lawson said 'like' not 'love'—and the difference is significant. As she felt his hands pushing back her skirt and sliding up her thighs, Cheska stepped back.

'And I'd like a glass of wine,' she told him chokily.

Lawson gave a wry smile. 'Coming up,' he said.

When he had poured their drinks, they carried them through to the sitting-room. Outside the day was fading in a symphony of translucent apricots, pinks and greys, so Cheska did not put on the light.

'You don't know how much Hatchford Manor will be valued at,' she said, sitting on the sofa, while Lawson stood in front of the fireplace, 'and it could be more than you anticipate.'

'I've a reasonable idea of what the valuation will be and I can afford it,' he replied, with the certainty of a man who has his hand on all the levers. 'I can also afford to have the house restored. Not to have all the work done immediately, but another couple of decent film successes will mean I have more than enough cash to cover it.'

After taking a sip of wine, Cheska tried another approach. 'Mightn't owning Hatchford Manor become an encumbrance?' she suggested. 'You've obviously moved around a lot over the past few years, spending periods of several months in the States, and managing a house of this size from a distance won't be easy.'

'But I don't intend to spend the rest of my days in perpetual motion,' Lawson told her. 'There's more to life than film, and——'

'Is that right?' Cheska said drily, before he could get any further. 'I understood it was the only reason you got up in the morning.'

He frowned across at her through the gathering gloom. 'It may have been at one time, but now—now I want to broaden my interests and also put down roots. My ideas aren't finalised, but I'm thinking along the lines of directing a major production which takes me abroad once a year, and spending the remainder of my time here.'

'Why not in Italy?' she asked.

'Because the English-speaking film industry is more wide-ranging and offers more opportunities than the Italian one, but also——' Lawson moved a hand '—because I like it here.'

'What would you do?' Cheska enquired.

'Make low-budget films which I'd both write and direct,' he said, starting to pace back and forth in front of the fireplace. 'I'm also interested in setting up a small film school which would offer courses in various aspects of the industry—and Hatchford Manor would make excellent premises.'

'It would also make an excellent place for afternoon teas,' she remarked.

Lawson stopped pacing. 'You don't want me to buy the manor,' he said.

'I'd prefer Rupert to keep it,' Cheska replied carefully. 'And he could, if he got busy with one of the ideas which I suggested. I'd help him. I'd run a tea-room myself.'

'Anything to keep me out,' he said, a bite to his voice. 'What is it with you? Why do you have to object? Why do you always have to be so bloody difficult?'

Cheska took another drink of wine. 'There are plenty of other manor houses in the south of England,' she said, in a level voice. 'Why not buy one of them?'

For a moment, Lawson studied the contents of his glass. 'Because I have no wish to.'

'But you could find something which is in better condition. And bigger, which would enable you to have a bigger film school,' she told him, smiling. 'Hatchford Manor only has eight bedrooms, so——'

'I'm buying the place,' he interjected.

Fear of his future proximity kicked at her stomach. 'What you expect, you get?' she demanded.

'Almost always,' Lawson responded.

Cheska's fingers tightened around the stem of her glass. She had tried logic, she had tried friendly persuasion—and he had rejected both. Why must he be so obstinate?

'From the start, your decision to direct a historical drama for television struck me as odd,' she declared, 'but now it's obvious that it was the house which was the deciding factor and the real draw.'

Lawson looked at her through the shadows. 'Is that so?'

'It is. You didn't film here by coincidence, you came because you knew Rupert was in financial difficulties and you saw an opportunity to make a killing.' Cheska rose to her feet. As she had been speaking, her fear had transformed itself into a fierce, if somewhat flustered anger; an anger which demanded she confront him. 'That's why you were so uptight when I told you that Rupert was my brother——'

'Uptight?' he said tersely.

'You almost threw a fit. And why you later asked if I part-owned the house,' Cheska continued. 'You thought that if I was a Finch and if I had a vested interest, some legal sway no matter how small, I'd be able to stop you.' She looked for a response, but he was gazing at her in silence, so she took a breath and hurried on. It was inexplicable, but she derived a certain piquancy, a *verve*, from battling with him. 'What did you do, plant the seed of selling in Rupert's head on your first visit and wait for it to ripen? Very astute! Well, now I know why you're so interested when we walk round the place, and how you come to know about listed buildings and——'

'Would you mind if I made three small observations?' Lawson cut in.

Cheska glowered. 'Go ahead.'

'One, I'd never set foot inside Hatchford Manor until I came to discuss filming, nor had I met your stepbrother, so I had no idea of his financial state. Two, I've agreed to pay the valuation price which, as the property market is currently depressed, it's doubtful the house would bring if it was put up for open sale. Three, as Rupert will confirm if you ask him, I've never so much as hinted at the possibility of his disposing of it,' he said, crisply demolishing her flimsily based argument.

Cheska frowned. She appeared to have wandered into the realms of fantasy and false accusations, and now she made a hasty attempt to correlate her thoughts.

'Even so, don't take it for granted that the purchase is incontrovertible,' she retaliated, using a word which she remembered him once using with her. 'Rupert has yet to sign on the dotted line and he could change his mind.'

'Don't you mean that you intend to do your damnedest to change it for him?' Lawson demanded. He had been calm, but all of a sudden he erupted in a burst of fiery Roman spirit. 'If you weren't so determined to view me as a bastard—though heaven knows why,' he rasped, 'you'd see that I'm doing Rupert a favour.'

'How kind!'

Lawson set down his wine glass on the stone mantle. As suddenly as his anger had come, it seemed to drain away. 'Cheska, as stimulating as annoying the hell out of each other can be, it——'

'Stimulating?' she cut in.

'Haven't you noticed how our arguments always contain a sexual element?' They did five years ago and they do now.'

Cheska thought back. Was he right and, if so, could this explain why, after what had seemed intensive battling, they had fallen straight into bed together?

'Maybe,' she muttered.

'There's no maybe about it,' Lawson replied. 'When we rowed over your car horn, you got me so turned on, so aroused I was this close——' his thumb and forefinger were held a quarter of an inch apart '—to dragging you down with me on to the ground, ripping off your clothes and penetrating you. And if I had, you'd have let me.' He came forward to remove the wine glass from her grasp and set it on the mantelpiece with his, then, catching hold of her hand, he drew her upright. 'But after a day when Miriam's incessant chatter has worn me out, I'm not in the mood for fighting. Besides, I can think of far more restful ways of us arousing each other. Like having a bath together, and me soaping your beautiful, beautiful breasts, and you soaping me, and——' He dropped a kiss on her forehead and turned them towards the door. 'Why am I wasting time just talking about it?'

Like hers, his bath was of the deep, roll-top Victorian type with shiny brass taps. It stood on clawed feet, to one side of the cork-floored, pine-walled, house-plant-cascading bathroom. When Cheska leaned back against Lawson, the water swirled warm and fragrant around her. Idiot, you should never have allowed him to bring you here, she told herself. But it's where I *need* to be, her other self replied. And tomorrow I will bolt the door. Tomorrow I will end this wonderful, this painful affair. Tomorrow...

As Lawson reached for a rose-scented tablet of soap and began to lather the globes of her breasts,

Cheska sighed. Her hair was caught up in a pile of dark tumbled curls on the top of her head, and as he caressed her he lowered his head and she felt the moistness of his mouth, the soft bite of his teeth, on her shoulder. His fingers slid through the bubbles and languorously caressed, on and on, until her breasts were swollen, their nipples stinging with desire.

'So pointed,' Lawson murmured, and as he pinched the tight peaks she gasped and arched her spine, a sudden spreading bursting need billowing inside her.

She moved around in the bath to face him. Kissing him, she soaped his shoulders, his chest, and when her hands slid beneath the water Lawson gave a low groan.

'Yes,' he said huskily, as she held him, massaged him, curled her fingers tight around the thrusting male power. Closing his eyes, Lawson threw back his dark head. His chest heaved and he sucked in a violent, shuddering, controlling breath. 'Oh, Cheska, *yes*.'

He pulled her to him, careless of the splashing water, to kiss her deeply, hungrily, urgently.

'Bed,' he instructed, the word hot against her mouth, and climbing out of the bath he dried himself on a thick white towel and then, with haste and fevered kisses, dried her.

His arm curved at her waist, Lawson led her through to his room and on to his bed. With great tenderness, he began kissing her in all the creases of her body, at her neck, her inner arm, the angles of her groin. The need between them mounted. Their breathing quickened. The bodies which had been damp from the bath became drenched with sweat. Placing a hand on his hip, Cheska steered him down until he lay on his back and then she straddled him. As she felt the thrust of him inside her, she moaned and bent forward, her swollen breasts reaching towards his mouth. Lawson suckled her and her body convulsed. Gripping her hips, he held her, steadied here, and together they began to move. Cheska shut her eyes. She was floating, adrift in a dark delirious world of pure sensation.

Sliding his hand down to where their thighs were locked, Lawson rubbed his thumb into the damp triangle of dark hair. As she felt his touch, Cheska gasped. His thumb moved again, caressing the hidden peak of pink flesh and in response to the searching rhythmic pressure, her body embraced him, enclosed him, drew him in deeper and deeper.

'Sweetheart,' Lawson groaned.

As his hands tightened on her thighs and his hips bucked against hers, Cheska gave herself up to driving need, to a scalding heat, and, in wildly flooding moment, to an abandonment which was incandescent and passionate and shook her to the very depths of her soul.

Some time later, Lawson stretched his arm over her and drew her close. 'Cheska,' he murmured drowsily. 'You and I together ... it's never been like this for me before ... the sex is fantastic.'

Cheska's heart shrivelled. She wanted to weep. She knew it was just a word, but she had not been having 'sex', she had been making love.

As Lawson settled into sleep, she lay still and pensive beside him. He might be intending to put down roots, but it would be foolish to think he would be interested in a meaningful relationship with her. Though even if he was, something crucial would be missing—legality. Cheska gazed bleakly out into the darkness. Lawson's reference to the joys of living in sin—and the fact that he had previously lived with someone—indicated that he would think in terms of what was basically a love affair, no matter if it was long-term. After all, such arrangements were commonplace within the entertainment world—within everyday life, come to that. But living together held no appeal. Cheska sighed. Maybe it was because her mother's marriages had been so happy, or simply because she needed security, but for her it had to be all—or nothing. Besides, in her mind, if you truly cared for someone then it meant you were prepared to commit yourself to them in every way, and that meant the exchange of marriage vows.

Cheska waited until Lawson's breathing became regular, then she slipped from under his arm, slid out of bed and tiptoed back through the door she had once intended to bolt. Every night she returned to her own bed. It might seem a small and pointless gesture, but it was the only sliver of independence she had to cling to and so, for her, it was important.

'It's been so good to know you,' Amy declared, throwing her arms around Cheska in a friendly farewell.

'And you,' she replied, with a smile.

'I hope we meet again some time. Bye.'

The actress was being given a lift to London by another member of the cast and Cheska went with them to the front door.

'Safe journey,' she said, waving.

Mid-afternoon, the final line of dialogue had been spoken and Lawson had declared that the film was 'a wrap'. He had gone on to invite the cast and crew to celebrate its finale with him, and so everyone had crowded into the library where drinks and a buffet which he had financed, and which Cheska and the canteen staff had arranged, was waiting. The mood had been one of euphoria. Everyone clearly believed that the production was destined to win accolades, become a benchmark, and was something they would be boasting about being connected with for years to come.

But now the party was over. For more than half an hour people had been coming to take their leave of her, and numbers were dwindling. A trio of technicians had arrived to remove items of film furniture and roll up carpets, but work on returning the house to its original state would not begin in earnest until the morning.

After saying goodbye to a few more of the crew, Cheska wandered into the drawing-room. The technicians had shown themselves to be conscientious, so she would not be overseeing the restoration process tomorrow. She gave a wry smile. In any case, as Lawson had not wavered in his intention to buy the house and, despite her continued plugging of her various schemes, Rupert still intended to sell it to him, if any damage should occur it would not be for her to worry about.

Cheska's chin tilted. If the worst came to the worst and her lover did become her permanent neighbour, she would not be worrying about that, either. In this life, you either rolled with things or let them roll over you and swamp you, and she had no intention of being swamped. What she would do was fall out of love with him. Cheska gave a strained smile. It was the only survival strategy she could think of. It wouldn't happen overnight nor be easy, but if she worked abroad again and didn't see Lawson for a couple of years, perhaps her addiction would wear off? She did not want to go overseas, and would be doing so *in extremis*, but desperate situations required desperate measures. She sighed. Admittedly her addiction had not worn off after five years, but she could meet someone else. She could, Cheska assured herself. And should her feelings prove not to be as gripping—well, there was nothing wrong with a more placid, less intense affection . . . was there?

'You haven't seen my photographs,' a drawling voice said, and Nicholas Preston strolled into the room.

'Photographs?' Cheska questioned.

'Of my daughter. I'm showing them to everyone before I depart.' He handed her a hefty cream leather album. 'What do you think?'

Opening the album, she looked down at a picture of a tiny wizened puce-faced baby swaddled in a white shawl and fast asleep.

Cheska grinned. 'She's nice.'

'Nice?' Nicholas protested. 'She's gorgeous. Small babies can be red and wrinkled and kind of plain, but not India-Jane. The kid who was brought along to play my son the other day was cute, but nowhere near as cute as her.'

'Jill enjoyed meeting you,' she told him.

He looked blank. 'Jill?'

'The baby's mother.'

'Oh...yah,' the actor said vaguely.

Cheska gave a wry smile. After being treated to a full fifteen minutes of his just-for-you gazes and ladykiller spiel, her friend had floated home on air, convinced she had wowed Nicholas Preston—but he appeared to have no recollection of the meeting.

'Look at this shot,' Nicholas instructed, turning the page to show her a picture of the baby with its face screwed up in a yawn and squinting drunkenly at the camera. 'Hasn't she got her daddy's eyes?'

'The same forget-me-not blue,' she said obligingly. As she was made to admire each snap in turn, Cheska cast the actor a glance. 'For someone who wasn't too keen on the joys of fatherhood, you seem to be very taken all of a sudden,' she could not resist saying.

Nicholas pouted, then grinned. 'So it took me a little time to realise what a charmer she is. But you're very taken with Lawson,' he said, as if in defence.

'I'm not,' Cheska protested.

'Honey, it's obvious that you dote on the guy, and always has been.'

She turned to the next page of photographs. 'Don't you mean that it's been obvious since you saw the video of the commercial?' she enquired tartly.

'The commercial?' Nicholas asked. 'What has that to do with anything?'

Cheska frowned. He seemed genuinely perplexed.

'Well,' she began hesitantly, 'it showed——'

'Showed what? You might think you've been keeping your feelings hidden, but to those of us who have an eye for such things they're easily detected—in the way you look at Lawson, how you speak to him, in just about everything. I knew you fancied him from day one.'

'You did?' she said, in astonishment.

'Couldn't avoid it,' Nicholas declared.

Cheska's brow puckered. The commercial had shown how well her face could mirror her emotions, but she had not realised she was still so transparent; especially when, in her own mind, she had spent the last six weeks determinedly playing the role of director's assistant. Period. She chewed at her lip. As someone who would view Lawson as competition and who depended on an awareness of body language for his living, Nicholas would be more perceptive than most, but how many other people had homed in on her feelings? Amy, for certain, but what about the other members of the cast and crew?

'Tell me about the commercial,' Nicholas said, as if sensing a story. 'What happened?'

'Nothing. Your daughter has your nose as well as your eyes,' Cheska declared.

Instantly distracted, the young man peered forward. 'You think so?' he said, and, accompanied by a long-winded account of India-Jane's eating, sleeping and bathtime habits, he proceeded to take her page by page through the remainder of the photographs.

'Your car'll have arrived,' Cheska told him, when, with the album tucked beneath his arm, Nicholas seemed about to march off in search of another victim. 'I'll come out with you. There are a couple of phone calls I need to make,' she explained.

'Cheerio, Lawson,' the actor called, as they passed the library where he was deep in a discussion with one of the cameramen.

He raised a hand. '*Ciao.*'

'Would you like to see——?' Nicholas began, opening the album.

'The car,' Cheska hissed, and she ushered him out to the yard where the cab driver was patiently waiting.

After bidding the actor goodbye, she continued on to her oast. Although the film was complete, there were a number of ends which she needed to tie up. Lifting the telephone, Cheska spoke first to the car hire company and then the Mayfly to ask if they would finalise their accounts and advising that she would be round to collect them the next morning.

The calls made, Cheska remained at her desk. She had refused to believe Lawson when he had said he'd not revealed the night they had spent together, she brooded, and she had been wrong. Could she have got other things wrong, too? Her gaze went out through the window, to where grey clouds were gathering on the horizon. If it rained, it would be for the first time in six weeks. Cheska frowned. She had dismissed Lawson's references to her hindrance during the time of the commercial, but——

Her mind went back and, for the first time in five years, she put the episode into clear focus. Rapt in thought, Cheska mulled over her behaviour, analysed it, passed judgement. Her grey eyes became troubled. She felt so *guilty*.

A movement outside the window caught her attention and when Cheska glanced up she saw Lawson coming from the direction of the manor house. He was obviously looking for her.

'I've been telephoning,' she explained, when she went to open the door. 'Is there something else you'd like me to do?'

Lawson shook his head. 'No, but the men will be finishing in another ten minutes or so and I thought you'd want to know so that you can go walkabout before locking up.'

'Thanks, I will.' Cheska frowned. 'But first I have an apology to make.'

'For what?'

'Come in,' she said, and when he had followed her into the sitting-room, she took a breath. 'For what happened five years ago.'

'And not before time!' Lawson rasped, in sudden explosive anger. 'I thought you were never going to explain, never going to——' a golden-skinned hand flew up into the air as he searched for the word '—repent. It seemed as if you intended to everlastingly pretend that the damned letter didn't happen.'

Cheska looked at him in bewilderment. 'Letter? What letter?' she asked.

'Don't act the innocent,' Lawson said impatiently. 'The one which you wrote giving me the brush-off.'

CHAPTER EIGHT

'THE brush off?' Cheska echoed.

'The big E, the cold shoulder, whatever the hell you want to call it. When I went into Delaneys' London office to give a quick courtesy report on the commercial before flying on to the States, your letter was handed to me,' Lawson said, his words curt and hard. 'Apparently you'd sent it down courier from Scotland to Justin Delaney, who'd handed it to a secretary, who passed it on to me.' His lip curled. 'Of course, it was sealed so there could be no danger of your boyfriend reading the contents, reading between the lines, and realising that we might have been lovers.'

'I don't know what you're talking about,' she said.

Lawson muttered something in Italian, something savage which sounded obscene. 'You can't have forgotten.'

'I never wrote any letter,' Cheska told him, and frowned. 'What did it say?'

'I tore the damn thing up, I was so bloody...wild,' he said testily, 'so I'm unable to recite it verbatim. But it was something about how while knowing me had been fun, it'd meant *niente*, nothing, and how your relationship with Justin meant everything. In other words, I rated as a fleeting entertainment, while he was the love of your life.' A nerve throbbed in his temple. 'It didn't exactly square with the fairy-tale you'd treated me to in Scotland, about how you'd ended what had always been a lacklustre alliance.'

'It wasn't a fairy-tale. It was the truth,' she protested.

'Yes?' Lawson said, the word wavering between disbelieving challenge and a query.

'*Yes*. Was the letter written or typed?' Cheska enquired.

'Written.'

'Can you remember what the writing looked like?'

Lawson's brow furrowed as he thought back. 'It was small—and square.'

'Whereas my writing is largish and loopy. You've seen it.'

His frown etched deeper. 'Yes, I have.'

'And I repeat, I did *not* write any letter,' Cheska said firmly.

In silence, he studied her. 'I believe you,' he said finally.

'Thanks!'

'But if you didn't write it, who did?' Lawson demanded, pushing his hands deep into his trouser pockets.

'It could've been Justin. *Was* Justin,' she asserted.

'Justin? But why? He didn't know about...us.'

Cheska sat down on the sofa. 'I think he did. Oh, he had no idea we'd spent the night together, but when he came up to Scotland I think he must have realised how I felt about you, even before I did myself.' She gave a thin smile. 'I appear to wear my heart very much on my sleeve. When I told

Justin that I resented being pushed into the commercial and that I wouldn't be seeing him again, he turned nasty,' she continued. 'He spoke of exacting retribution, giving me my come-uppance and wreaking his revenge.'

'Shades of a Victorian melodrama,' Lawson remarked drily.

She nodded. 'It would have been funny, if he hadn't been so vicious, so malicious. Afterwards I decided he'd just been sounding off, and when time passed and nothing happened, I forgot about it. But now—well, he seems to have struck back by trying to undermine any possible romance between us.'

Though Justin had not just undermined, he had killed their romance stone-dead, Cheska thought, her stomach churning as the consequences of the young man's spite, the realisation of what could have been—if only—hit home.

Lawson looked sombre. 'You resented being pushed into the commercial?' he demanded.

She nodded. 'My inclusion had been fixed without my knowing anything about it, without my being consulted,' she told him, and went on to explain about her relationship with Justin and how, when she had been set to say they were through, the young man had announced that he had arranged for her to appear in his father's advertisement. 'Justin expected me to fall at his feet slobbering my gratitude, but I was annoyed; not because I considered myself above appearing in the commercial—I didn't—but because I felt manipulated . . . and hemmed in.'

'Couldn't you have got out of it?'

'How?' Cheska implored. 'Justin had told his father that I was desperate to take part and so, as far as Mr Delaney was concerned, by pulling strings and insisting on my inclusion he'd done me a great favour. But, also, the shoot had been organised and if I'd pulled out it would have meant a delay and caused all kinds of trouble to all kinds of people.'

Lawson sat down at the opposite end of the sofa. 'But you caused trouble anyway. You caused *me* trouble.'

'Lots.'

His brows lifted. 'You agree?'

'I do, and that was what I wanted to apologise for.' Cheska paused for a moment, assembling her thoughts. 'Because as an adolescent I'd always been allowed to go my own sweet way, because I was a wilful little brat, if anyone rattled me—as Justin Delaney had rattled me—my reaction was to become——'

'Bloody minded and uncooperative?' Lawson provided.

She heaved a sigh. 'Yes, though I never realised just how irritating I obviously was.'

'And, being pretty, you must have got away with murder.'

'I guess,' Cheska acknowledged. 'But whatever I did, whatever I said, Rupert didn't object, which made it difficult for me to gauge when I was going too far. So I grumbled about the clothes I was to wear for the commercial, and I complained about the rain which delayed the shoot and kept us in Scotland for more than a week, and——'

'You arrived late for everything, and you flounced out of the house instead of elegantly strode, and you repeatedly climbed into the car at the wrong angle, and——'

'I went all out to hinder,' Cheska summed up, then added a touch defensively, 'but you made everything so much worse.'

'I did?' Lawson protested. 'How?'

'You were the first person I'd met who obstructed me, with any real force, and I was damned if I'd let you control me.'

'I guess my reaction to you rattling me was to *over*react,' he mused, plucking at his lower lip with his fingers. 'I ought never to have stormed; I should have coaxed, reasoned. But you'd wound me up tight——' Lawson hesitated, and when he continued it appeared to be in a different direction '—and the production seemed so vital. The commercials I made were never merely commercials to me, they were five-finger exercises in filmmaking,' he told her. 'They were my apprenticeship before I moved on to directing something bigger and, at the time of the car commercial, I was about to do just that. After seeing examples of my work, the chief executive of an American film company had asked me to fly over to discuss directing my first movie. He'd also told me to bring along tapes of all the commercials I'd done, including the last one.'

Her grey eyes large and dismayed, Cheska looked at him along the length of the sofa. 'You mean your future hinged on whether or not he approved of the car commercial?' she asked.

'That's what it seemed like at the time, though now I realise I took it far too seriously. Even if the commercial had been a bummer——'

'Even if I'd ruined it!' she inserted.

'—my track record would have seen me through, because as soon as we started to talk it became clear that the guy had already decided to give me my chance.'

Guilt gnawed in the pit of her stomach. Cheska felt dreadful. 'I'm so sorry,' she said; 'it never occurred to me that I could be wrecking things for you.'

'You didn't,' Lawson said.

'I might have done. I was so busy being the peeved, resentful, self-centred child!' Cheska muttered, in a fierce condemnation of her earlier self.

'But you've matured beautifully, and I don't just mean your looks,' he told her.

She frowned. 'I should hope so.'

'You have,' Lawson insisted. 'Why was Rupert so indulgent towards you?' he went on. 'All right, he felt bad about his sister——' Lawson paused, looking out at the dark clouds which were growing and moving slowly forward '—and he's the kind of guy who'd settle for peace at almost any price, but even so——'

'He also felt bad about what had happened to me when I was younger.'

'What did happen?' he asked.

Cheska's brows drew together. 'First of all, when I was eight my father died. My parents had been married for ages and were desperate for a baby by the time I was born and perhaps because of that we were a particularly close and loving family. So when Dad suffered a coronary, it was——' She hesitated. Even after all this time, the memory was still painful. 'His death hit me hard and he left a huge gap.'

Stretching out his arm, Lawson touched her fingers. 'I understand how you feel. I never knew my mother, but even so——' He broke off and sat back. 'Carry on,' he said.

'A couple of years later when my mother met Desmond Finch and they decided to get married, I was delighted. I liked Desmond and he liked me, and, although I didn't regard him as a replacement for my father, their marriage meant that the gap was starting to close. I liked Rupert, too,' Cheska added.

'When your mother and Desmond were married, did he live at Hatchford Manor as well?' he enquired.

'No; although it was his home base, for the twelve months of their marriage he was away in the jungles of South America, tracking down the habitat of some rare butterfly.'

'The marriage only lasted for a year?' Lawson frowned. 'Were they divorced?'

'No! They were devoted to each other. But one day——'

Cheska stopped. Her throat had stiffened and she could feel the hot sting of tears at the back of her eyes.

'One day what?' he prompted gently.

She swallowed. 'It was a beautiful Sunday in the spring and we were driving down to the coast for the day,' she said, speaking quickly. 'My mother was beside Desmond in the front of the car, and I was in the back. We were travelling happily along, all three of us were singing, when a lorry shot out of a side road. It sliced into the front of the car, spinning us around, and we crashed into a tree, bounced off to plough up several yards of hedge, and eventually came to rest on the verge. Everything had happened so quickly and been so noisy, but now there was complete silence.' Cheska swallowed again. 'I sat there frozen, looking at my mother and Desmond who were slumped in their seats. They were still, but, all of a sudden, Mum stretched out her hand and made a choking sound—and then she died.'

'Desmond was already dead?'

She bowed her head. 'I didn't know it at the time, but yes.'

'Oh, Cheska,' Lawson murmured, and moving along the sofa, he put his arms around her. 'Were you hurt?' he asked.

'No, that was the amazing part. I didn't have a scratch, a bruise, and afterwards it made me feel so guilty. My mother and Desmond had both suffered massive internal injuries, yet I was untouched.'

'Physically,' he said.

Cheska gave a weak smile. 'Yes. When Rupert was notified, he flew straight back from South America,' she continued, 'and by the time he arrived I was trying to be brave and so I bottled up my grief. I did it by blocking the accident from my mind and refusing to talk about it.'

'Rupert didn't attempt to persuade you to talk?'

She shook her head. 'The current wisdom is that he ought to have done, but he just let me be. Whether that made any difference or not, I don't know, but it took me a long time to come to terms. For years I had nightmares when I'd see my mother raise her hand and hear her choking again.'

'And I once said that your life was a bed of roses,' Lawson muttered, and held her closer.

For a moment, Cheska rested against his shoulder, then she drew away. Whilst she was grateful for his sympathy, a part of her remained wary of being held in his arms.

'Whatever's happened and even though Rupert may not have acted as wisely as he should, I've been very fortunate in that he looked after me, brought me up, and he loves me,' she said.

'Did he become a surrogate father?'

Cheska gave a small smile. 'No. He was in his late thirties when he took me on so he could have done, but half the time it seemed to be me who made the decisions.'

Lawson arched a brow. 'Which doesn't surprise me. And now he has Miriam to make decisions for him.'

She grinned. 'Yes. It's funny,' she went on reflectively, 'but as I blocked off the accident, so I also blocked the commercial from my mind. I think that, deep down, I've always felt guilty about my behaviour, though I wasn't prepared to admit it.' Cheska's brow puckered. 'There's something else I want to apologise for—my attempts to persuade Rupert to keep Hatchford Manor and so prevent you from buying it. I—I had my reasons, but the best thing which could happen to the house would be for you to become the new owner.'

'You mean that?' he demanded.

'I mean it.' She cast him a look. 'Though you're determined to buy, come hell or high water, and regardless of anything which I might say.'

'Correct.' Lawson's brown eyes held hers. 'And as we're into true confessions, I'll tell you why I'm so determined. It's because of my mother.'

'Your mother?' Cheska said, in bewilderment.

'I'm buying Hatchford Manor, her home, for her. She may have been thrown out of it when she was alive, but, in death, I'm returning it to her.'

She stared at him. 'You mean that—that your mother was Sylvie Finch?' she faltered.

Lawson nodded. 'I do. She was.'

A pool of silence formed. Outside, the grey clouds darkened and rolled nearer, a pair of green woodpeckers headed homewards, a sudden gust of wind rifled through the branches of the trees.

'Rupert is your uncle,' Cheska said.

'Yes. And when you told me that he was your brother, I thought it meant that——' Lawson blew out a breath '—that when I'd made love to you I'd made love to my aunt.'

She gave a startled laugh. 'So that's why you were so uptight.'

'And so relieved when you revealed that he was only your stepbrother.'

'Miriam said she thought you and Rupert had similar traits,' Cheska recalled.

Lawson looked surprised. 'Do you think that we do?'

'No, though——' she would need to give the matter further consideration '—perhaps. So it was your father who didn't meet with Beatrice Finch's approval,' she continued.

Lawson nodded. 'He'd come over to England to learn the language and was working in a local restaurant, and I imagine she regarded him as the stereotypical Italian waiter.'

'Which was no reason to go berserk,' Cheska protested.

'None,' he agreed, 'and had she been able to see into the future she most certainly wouldn't have done. On his return to Italy, my father opened a *trattoria* of his own, then a couple more, and when they were successful he branched out and bought a hotel. Now he owns a chain of luxury hotels spread throughout the country, plus a couple in the States, and he's wealthy, respected and a man of repute.'

'So boo to you, Beatrice Finch!'

Lawson grinned. 'Or something similar.'

'When you met Rupert, why didn't you tell him who you were?' Cheska enquired, sobering.

'Because I was uncertain of the reception I'd get. He seemed amiable, but if I'd suddenly announced that I was his nephew he could have cut up rough. After all, I've been reared on tales of the fearsome Beatrice and, although my father reckoned Rupert was a pussycat, as he got older he could have become a tiger.'

'Did you know that Rupert had stuck up for Sylvie—your mother?'

'Yes, though I wanted to hear your version. But I wasn't aware, nor is my father, of the role which Desmond played. I'm afraid we'd marked him down as one of the bad guys.'

'Whereas Sylvie's departure was a great sorrow to him,' Cheska brooded.

'How did he and Beatrice get along together afterwards?' Lawson enquired.

'Not well. He would have left her, but shortly after she'd despatched Sylvie she was diagnosed as suffering from cancer. Beatrice lived for another two or three years, but Desmond told my mother that it was a relief when she died, because he couldn't forgive her. He always mourned the loss of Sylvie—and you.'

Lawson heaved a sigh. 'Which makes it seem tragic now that my father didn't keep a line of communication open,' he reflected. 'But my mother had been so hurt and he was proud, and he swore he wanted nothing more to do with the Finch family.'

'But you did,' Cheska said.

'Yes, when I was a child I made my father tell me everything he could about my mother, and where she'd lived. I guess it's genes or something, but I always felt drawn here, which is why I applied to attend university in Sussex.'

She tilted her head. 'What was your father's reaction?'

'He didn't approve, but he understood.'

'Did you take a look at Hatchford Manor during your time here?' Cheska asked curiously.

Lawson nodded. 'I used to come on my motorbike, stop on the hill opposite, and gaze across. I concocted all kinds of excuses for knocking on the door, but always chickened out at the last moment.'

'I might have answered the door,' she said.

'And been a little madam,' he told her, grinning.

Cheska made a face at him.

'However,' Lawson continued, 'earlier this year, when I heard that a film was to be made here and the original director had dropped out——' He grinned again. 'It would have taken wild horses to keep me away. And when we met again I didn't tell *you* who I was, because you were an unknown quantity. Don't forget, as far as I knew you'd ditched me!'

'Ditto,' Cheska said. 'You'd promised faithfully to get in touch, but I never heard a thing.'

'You gave me an address and telephone number in London,' he recalled.

'It was a bedsit which I rented at the time. But if I'd said Hatchford Manor was my home——' She looked at him.

'The course of history would have been changed, in one way or another,' Lawson said pithily. 'When you didn't hear from me, you could have got in touch,' he pointed out.

'I know, but——'

'You weren't all that keen?'

'I was keen. Very keen. I was——' Cheska stopped short. She had been about to blurt out that she had loved him, but wouldn't she be in danger of making a fool of herself? Lawson might have been hurt at being ditched, as he had imagined, but it did not necessarily mean he had cared for her. Cared deeply. 'I knew very little about you, the kind of man you were,' Cheska said, her tone calmer and aiming for matter-of-fact, 'so I had no way of knowing whether or not you'd regarded what had happened between us as . . . serious.'

'And not knowing me is why you decided that I'd slept with you because I was attempting to wring an appropriate performance out of you?' Lawson enquired.

'Well . . . yes.'

He raked back the dark hair which spilled over his brow. 'It wasn't. When I suggested we have a drink together in my room and talk, my sole intention was to try and persuade you to drop the hostility and be amenable. Remember, earlier, how I said you'd wound me up tight?' he enquired, going off at a tangent. Cheska nodded. 'As you'd resented being pushed into the part, so I was riled that I hadn't been allowed any say, so before we met I was all set to disapprove of this girl who'd been given a role in my commercial simply because she was the dealer's son's girlfriend.'

'Which was understandable.'

'Maybe,' Lawson agreed, 'but when I saw you, I thought you were perfect for the part and perfect for me.'

An unbidden smile came to her lips, though Cheska quickly banished it. 'Perfect for you?' she asked.

'Yes, and I found it maddening.'

'Why?'

'Because at that time I was touched with burning ambition, and having a women enter my life—a woman who was not prepared to be docile—would've complicated everything.'

Cheska grinned. 'You didn't consider I'd be docile?'

'No way, and you rapidly proved me right,' Lawson responded grittily.

'So you suggested we talk with the idea of making me amenable,' she said, returning the conversation to what he had formerly been saying.

'Yes, but everything went a little crazy and all of a sudden we were locked mouth to mouth.'

'And you had the look which you required from me the next morning,' Cheska observed.

'I did,' Lawson agreed, 'but while the professional side of me was delighted, it was—by the way.'

'Why were you reluctant to show me the video?' she asked quizzically.

'Because I hadn't played it for years, and when I played it to Amy it'd brought everything sharply back and I'd found it painful. My mother apart,' he continued, 'there's another reason why I want to—why I *shall*—buy Hatchford Manor. You.'

'Me?' Cheska protested.

Lawson gave a curt nod. 'You may not be prepared to commit yourself to a relationship yet, but given time you will. Think about it, Cheska,' he said, his voice picking up an urgency. 'If you hadn't made love in five years but you made love to me, then it must mean——'

'Not prepared to commit myself?' she interrupted.

'Every night you go back to your own damn bed,' he said, raising two anguished fists. 'You've never *ever* let us wake up together, so——'

'Are you prepared to commit yourself?' Cheska enquired.

'You bet!' Lawson shot back. 'I want to marry you, like tomorrow. How's that?'

When the unbidden smile tugged at her lips again, this time she let it stay. And with the smile, came a deliciously warm feeling inside her.

'Sounds like commitment to me,' she replied.

'So why have you deserted me every night?' he asked austerely.

'Because I thought that, sooner or later, you'd walk away,' Cheska explained, 'and I had to retain something. Some pride. I couldn't give you *everything* of me.'

'I'm not going to walk away,' Lawson protested. 'I love you.'

Her smile grew. It widened her mouth, it lightened her eyes, it added a glow to her skin.

'You love me?' Cheska said, savouring the phrase and hugging it close to her heart.

'Truly, madly, deeply,' he vowed.

'And I love you. Truly, madly, deeply,' she told him.

Lawson's mouth curved. 'Which is why the sex, our lovemaking, has always been so terrific,' he said. 'Us caring for each other was the vital ingredient which makes all the difference.'

Cheska gave her agreement. 'I said I had my reasons for not wanting you to buy Hatchford Manor,' she reminded him. 'It was because I loved you, and I couldn't resist you, and I had visions of myself being tied hopelessly into a love affair for years and years to come.'

'You're going to be tied into a love affair for years and years to come,' he told her, 'so long as you agree to be my wife.'

'I do,' Cheska said.

Lawson grinned. 'What, no objection?'

'None.'

Moving closer, he kissed her, and as she felt the heat of his mouth Cheska clutched at him, her fingers sliding down his chest to curl around the rough width of his leather belt. They kissed again, and as she felt him stir against her she became aware

of the unmistakable effect she was having on him—
and the effect he was having on her.

'I have to lock up the house,' Cheska said, a little
shakily.

Raising her hand to his mouth, Lawson nibbled
at the fleshy base of her thumb. 'Now? Can't it
wait?' he protested.

'It could, but——' her gaze went outside to the
steel grey sky '—it looks as if it's getting ready to
rain.'

He made a conscious effort to bank down his
desire. 'Then we'd better go.'

The workmen had departed and the furniture
they had removed had left the manor looking a little
forlorn. But not for long, Cheska thought.

'We can live in one of the oasts while the reno-
vations are being done,' she said, as they did the
rounds of the upper floor. 'Or have the oasts made
into one and live there permanently, and give the
manor over in total to your film school.'

'Or we could have seven kids and find other
premises for it,' Lawson said, drawing her close.

'Seven?' Cheska wrinkled her nose. 'I reckon
living in the oasts and having a couple would be
better.'

He grinned. 'Your choice,' he said.

'How do you know about listed buildings?' she
asked, when the rooms had been checked and they
were walking down the stairs.

'Because, when I saw the state of things here, I
started to think of ways in which repairs could be
financed,' Lawson explained, 'and I made a few
enquiries—for Rupert's benefit.'

'I don't think he'd have been interested,' she said, 'as I don't think he was ever really interested in my schemes. In fact, I suspect he could have been considering selling and marrying Miriam for a while, but he needed time to pluck up his courage to propose.' Cheska shone a mischievous grin. 'How do you fancy a double wedding?'

Lawson groaned and pretended he needed to cling on to the bannister in order to keep upright. 'Sounds like a fate worse than death!'

'When Rupert realises that you're Sylvie's son, he might feel that you're entitled to part of the value of the house,' she said suddenly.

'Out of the question. I'm paying the full price.'

'But——'

'Everything which is Rupert's will eventually be passed on to you,' Lawson declared, and pulling her close he plucked kisses from her lips. 'My wife.'

'You were so cool and detached on the set,' Cheska commented, when, after a few minutes, they embarked on their tour of the ground floor.

'It was the only way I could function. I knew that if I'd smiled at you for a moment too long, if I'd had one touch of your hand, I'd have forgotten about the film and turned into a twitching, slavering lovesick slave.'

She laughed. 'I'd have liked that.'

'I bet you would,' Lawson said, and hauling her into the lean angles of his body, he gave her several more kisses.

'Do I make you jealous?' Cheska asked, when she had caught her breath.

'Pea green. Why do you think I was so furious when I found you lunching with Nicholas?'

She left him to check a window-lock. 'It wasn't because you feared for the smooth running of the film?' she enquired, smiling back over her shoulder.

'It was because the thought of him laying so much as one finger on your beautiful silken flesh made me want to tear the guy limb from limb,' Lawson informed her. 'Has everything been given your seal of approval?'

'It has.'

'Thank heavens,' he said. 'Now we can get back to what really matters.'

'Oh, dear!' Cheska exclaimed, when he opened the front door.

It was pouring down; the rain slewed from a gun-metal dark sky in determined diagonals and was bouncing off the ground.

'At least it waited until we'd finished the film,' Lawson observed thankfully.

'But it didn't wait that extra five minutes until we could get back to the oasts!'

'Would you like a fireman's lift over my shoulder?' he enquired.

Cheska grinned. 'No, thanks, I'll just run.'

The alarm was set, the door locked, then, hand in hand and with heads bent against the driving rain, they set off, splashing through puddles, skidding across the shiny cobbles of the yard, brushing past dripping bushes, until they reached her oast.

'Yuck!' Cheska complained, lifting a sodden hank of hair from her eyes and plucking at her drenched T-shirt and jeans.

'Yuck nothing,' Lawson declared, and gave a low growl. 'You look *bella*.'

Raising his hands, he circled his palms on the peaks of her breasts which were pushing up the wet cotton. Cheska's heart began to pump.

'Why don't we take off our clothes, have a bath and go to bed?' she suggested breathlessly.

'We'll miss out the bath,' Lawson told her. 'And before we go to bed, you have to promise me something—that when we go to bed tonight you'll still be with me in the morning.'

His palms were moving relentlessly over her nipples, the room had begun to swim, and she was finding it difficult to stand still.

'I promise,' Cheska gasped.

'Then let's go,' Lawson said, and drew her with him up the stairs.

'What's the rush?' she asked, when he had deftly undressed her and himself, and they were lying, limbs tangled around limbs, beneath the duvet.

'Cheska, we have five years to catch up on.'

'And the rest of our lives together,' she said dreamily.

'For certain, but do you think my lady could stop talking?' Lawson demanded.

Cheska wrapped her arms around his neck. She liked him calling her 'my lady'. It meant that she was loved, and she was cherished, she belonged to Lawson. *Her* man.

'Your lady could,' she replied, and kissed him, and for a long time the only sound was the pattering of the rain on the windows.

BRIDE'S BAY RESORT

UNLOCK THE DOOR TO GREAT ROMANCE AT BRIDE'S BAY RESORT

Join Harlequin's new across-the-lines series, set in an exclusive hotel on an island off the coast of South Carolina.

Seven of your favorite authors will bring you exciting stories about fascinating heroes and heroines discovering love at Bride's Bay Resort.

Look for these fabulous stories coming to a store near you beginning in January 1996.

Harlequin American Romance #613 in January
Matchmaking Baby by Cathy Gillen Thacker

Harlequin Presents #1794 in February
Indiscretions by Robyn Donald

Harlequin Intrigue #362 in March
Love and Lies by Dawn Stewardson

Harlequin Romance #3404 in April
Make Believe Engagement by Day Leclaire

Harlequin Temptation #588 in May
Stranger in the Night by Roseanne Williams

Harlequin Superromance #695 in June
Married to a Stranger by Connie Bennett

Harlequin Historicals #324 in July
Dulcie's Gift by Ruth Langan

Visit Bride's Bay Resort each month wherever Harlequin books are sold.

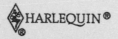 HARLEQUIN ®

BBAYG

MILLION DOLLAR SWEEPSTAKES
AND
EXTRA BONUS PRIZE DRAWING

No purchase necessary. To enter the sweepstakes, follow the directions published and complete and mail your Official Entry Form. If your Official Entry Form is missing, or you wish to obtain an additional one (limit: one Official Entry Form per request, one request per outer mailing envelope) send a separate, stamped, self-addressed #10 envelope (4 1/8" X 9 1/2") via first-class mail to: Million Dollar Sweepstakes and Extra Bonus Prize Drawing Entry Form, P.O. Box 1867, Buffalo, NY 14269-1867. Request must be received no later than January 15, 1998. For eligibility into the sweepstakes, entries must be received no later than March 31,1998. No liability is assumed for printing errors, lost, late, non-delivered or misdirected entries. Odds of winning are determined by the number of eligible entries distributed and received.

Sweepstakes open to residents of the U.S. (except Puerto Rico), Canada and Europe who are 18 years of age or older. All applicable laws and regulations apply. Sweepstakes offer void wherever prohibited by law. Values of all prizes are in U.S. currency. This sweepstakes is presented by Torstar Corp., its subsidiaries and affiliates, in conjunction with book, merchandise and/or product offerings. For a copy of the Official Rules governing this sweepstakes, send a self-addressed, stamped envelope (WA residents need not affix return postage) to: MILLION DOLLAR SWEEP-STAKES AND EXTRA BONUS PRIZE DRAWING Rules, P.O. Box 4470, Blair, NE 68009-4470, USA.

FAST CASH 4033 DRAW RULES
NO PURCHASE OR OBLIGATION NECESSARY

Fifty prizes of $50 each will be awarded in random drawings to be conducted no later than 6/28/96 from amongst all eligible responses to this prize offer received as of 5/14/96. To enter, follow directions, affix 1st-class postage and mail OR write Fast Cash 4033 on a 3" x 5" card along with your name and address and mail that card to: Harlequin's Fast Cash 4033 Draw, P.O. Box 1395, Buffalo, NY 14240-1395 OR P.O. Box 618, Fort Erie, Ontario L2A 5X3. (Limit: one entry per outer envelope; all entries must be sent via 1st-class mail.) Limit: one prize per household. Odds of winning are determined by the number of eligible responses received. Offer is open only to residents of the U.S. (except Puerto Rico) and Canada and is void wherever prohibited by law. All applicable laws and regulations apply. Any litigation within the province of Quebec respecting the conduct and awarding of a prize in this sweepstakes may be submitted to the Régie des alcools, des courses et des jeux. In order for a Canadian resident to win a prize, that person will be required to correctly answer a time-limited arithmetical skill-testing question to be administered by mail. Names of winners available after 7/30/96 by sending a self-addressed, stamped envelope to: Fast Cash 4033 Draw Winners, P.O. Box 4200, Blair, NE 68009-4200.

SWP-H3ZD

You're About to Become a

Become a

Privileged Woman

Reap the rewards of fabulous free gifts and
benefits with proofs-of-purchase from
Harlequin and Silhouette books

Pages & Privileges™

It's our way of thanking you for
buying our books at your
favorite retail stores.

✂

**PROOF OF
PURCHASE**

HP-PP112

Offer expires October 31, 1996

Harlequin and Silhouette—
the most privileged readers in the world!

For more information about Harlequin and
Silhouette's PAGES & PRIVILEGES program call the
Pages & Privileges Benefits Desk: 1-503-794-2499

❖ HARLEQUIN®

HP-PP112